DEATH OF
AN AUTHOR

DEATH OF AN AUTHOR

E. C. R. Lorac

with an introduction by
MARTIN EDWARDS

This edition first published in 2023 by
The British Library
96 Euston Road
London NW1 2DB

Death of an Author was first published in
1935 by Sampson Low, London.

Introduction © 2023 Martin Edwards
Death of an Author © 1935 The Estate of E.C.R. Lorac
Volume Copyright © The British Library Board

Cataloguing in Publication Data

A catalogue record for this publication is
available from the British Library

ISBN 978 0 7123 5467 7
e-ISBN 978 0 7123 6840 7

Front cover image © The London Picture Archive

Text design and typesetting by Tetragon, London
Printed in England by TJ Books, Padstow, Cornwall

CONTENTS

INTRODUCTION

Death of an Author is a rare example of a novel by E.C.R. Lorac (the principal pen name of Carol Rivett) that does not feature her popular and long-serving series detective Inspector Macdonald. The story is so entertaining, however, that we don't miss him, especially given that Lorac introduces an appealing and capable pair of substitute investigators in Chief Inspector Warner of the CID and Inspector Bond.

The novel, originally published in 1935, boasts an unorthodox and well-crafted plot, but is particularly strong in its depiction of the literary world of the mid-1930s. This is a subject which evidently fascinated Lorac, and she returned to it more than once in subsequent novels, including *These Names Make Clues*, which has been republished as a British Library Crime Classic. Here, the opening scenes are especially pleasing and one can almost taste the relish with which she wrote them.

The story opens with an encounter between Andrew Marriott, a publisher, and his star author Michael Ashe, whose successes have made him a celebrity. They have a wonderful exchange in which Ashe threatens to write a crime novel, only for Marriott to respond: "Crime stories are a legitimate branch of fiction, but they're mere ephemerals—selling like hot cakes today, and gone tomorrow."

This view was widely held at the time, not least by many of those who wrote detective fiction. Among Lorac's contemporaries, the poet Cecil Day-Lewis (whose mysteries were published under the name Nicholas Blake) and the broadcaster and priest Ronald Knox, undoubtedly regarded their whodunits as ephemeral, although Day-Lewis soon came to appreciate—and exploit—the literary potential of the genre. Even Agatha Christie gave spoilers about the solutions to four of her early mysteries in *Cards on the Table*, an Hercule Poirot novel of 1936, which suggests that she thought they had passed their sell-by date. Today, such modesty seems wholly misplaced.

Everything I've learned while researching Lorac over the years leads me to the conclusion that she had a stout belief in the value of her work, although no doubt she would have been not only thrilled but also amazed by the sales figures (and positive reviews) her books have achieved as a result of appearing in the Crime Classics series.

The conversation between Marriott and Ashe turns to a novel written by another of Marriott's authors. The book in question is *The Charterhouse Case* by Vivian Lestrange. As Ashe says, Lestrange has "achieved the impossible—or at least, the improbable—by writing a crime story that is in the rank of first rate novels. His writing, his characterisation, and his situations all disarm criticism."

Lestrange, it seems, is a recluse who refuses to have his photograph taken for publicity purposes and about whom nothing is known. Marriott and Ashe debate whether a book of such quality could really be the work of a newcomer and also the extent to which the authenticity of the prison life background of the story is such that it must be based on real life experience rather than simply meticulous research. Marriott concedes that: "to do them justice, some of the 'thriller merchants' take an infinite amount of trouble to get their facts vetted. The standard is going up steadily..."

Ashe persuades his publisher to arrange a dinner party at which he can meet the mysterious Lestrange. But a shock is in store. We are told that Lestrange is actually a young woman. Marriott regards her as "the coolest creature I ever met in my life!"

What follows is interesting and relevant to the storyline and it also gives us an intriguing insight into Lorac's attitude towards the treatment of female writers by reviewers and the publishing industry generally. On first meeting the young woman, Marriott said, "I have been flattering myself for years that I could tell a man's writing from a woman's..." Her response is blunt: "I get so sick of that theory. The minute a reviewer learns from some gossip that so and so is a woman, he promptly writes 'there is a touch of femininity about the writings of X.Y.Z. Her descriptions are above criticism, but her dialogue betrays her sex.' It's all my eye and Betty Martin!"

When Ashe—accompanied by Marriott and his colleague Bailley—meets the young woman, he is thunderstruck. She is scathing: "What but male conceit formulated that judgment of yours that no woman could have written a book which you admired? Is your estimate of all women the same?" She also makes a forceful case for equal treatment: "You envisage women still as the sheltered, emotional playthings of men. The woman of today is beginning to see through the fraud... We are still handicapped by the habit of thought of centuries, still too prone to acknowledge the unique splendour of the gifted male—but your 'weaker vessel' theory—I deride it!"

Three months after that dinner party, however, a woman walks into Hampstead Police Station to announce that she is afraid that something has happened to Vivian Lestrange. The author is missing from home and so is the housekeeper.

The elaborate mystery which gradually unfolds tests the detective skills of Warner and Bond, but they rise to the challenge. To say much more without giving too many spoilers is almost impossible, but although this has until now been a vanishingly rare book, most people lucky enough to read it in modern times have been greatly impressed.

Warner (who hates the idea of hanging and favours abolition: hardly a conventional view for policemen of his era) and Bond are a likeable duo. One minor mystery is why Lorac abandoned them after this novel. Perhaps the explanation lies in the fact that this was the last novel of hers published by Sampson Low. She moved to the more prestigious Collins Crime Club imprint, and it may well be that, since Macdonald was already a well-established series character, the publishers were keen for the author to make the most of him.

Edith Caroline Rivett (1894–1958), generally known as Carol Rivett, published her first detective novel in 1931. There can be little doubt—as the discussion in this book makes clear—that she adopted the ambiguous writing name of E.C.R. Lorac because of a suspicion of prejudice against female authors. She was so successful in hiding her identity that, many years later, the crime novelist and critic Harry Keating wrote of his astonishment at discovering, eventually, that she was a woman.

She wasn't alone in fearing prejudice. In *The Life of Crime: Detecting the History of Mysteries and Their Creators*, I've discussed other female authors who masqueraded as men, notably Elizabeth Mackintosh (who was better known as Josephine Tey but whose first detective novel appeared under the name Gordon

Daviot) and Lucy Malleson (who wrote most of her mysteries under the name Anthony Gilbert). Even Agatha Christie toyed, briefly, with the idea of adopting a masculine pseudonym. By 1936, however, Carol Rivett was confident enough to create a new literary identity using her own first name, and so was born Carol Carnac. One of the Carnac titles, *Crossed Skis*, has so far been reprinted as a British Library Crime Classic.

How it must have amused her to put these words in Warner's mouth: "If I petitioned Parliament, do you think I could get an enactment that no man writes under any name but his own, and his finger-prints be registered on the title page?" When Bond points out that some writers produce different kinds of work under a host of different names, Warner groans: "Hardened offenders… recidivists, I call 'em."

Late in life Carol Rivett used a further pen name, Mary Le Bourne, when writing *Two-Way Murder*. That book, however, did not find its way into print for more than sixty years prior to first publication in the Crime Classics series under the E.C.R. Lorac pen name. That is yet another good example of the strange and unpredictable nature of the author's life, a subject right at the heart of this lively novel.

MARTIN EDWARDS
www.martinedwardsbooks.com

A NOTE FROM THE PUBLISHER

The original novels and short stories reprinted in the British Library Crime Classics series were written and published in a period ranging, for the most part, from the 1890s to the 1960s. There are many elements of these stories which continue to entertain modern readers; however, in some cases there are also uses of language, instances of stereotyping and some attitudes expressed by narrators or characters which may not be endorsed by the publishing standards of today. We acknowledge therefore that some elements in the works selected for reprinting may continue to make uncomfortable reading for some of our audience. With this series British Library Publishing aims to offer a new readership a chance to read some of the rare books of the British Library's collections in an affordable paperback format, to enjoy their merits and to look back into the world of the twentieth century as portrayed by its writers. It is not possible to separate these stories from the history of their writing and as such the following stories are presented as they were originally published with the inclusion of minor edits made for consistency of style and sense, and with pejorative terms of an extremely offensive nature partly obscured. We welcome feedback from our readers, which can be sent to the following address:

British Library Publishing
The British Library
96 Euston Road
London, NW1 2DB
United Kingdom

CHAPTER I

ANDREW MARRIOTT, MANAGING DIRECTOR OF LANGSTON'S, the publishers, was often heard to say that thirty years' experience of writers had given him so much insight into their peculiar mentality that he had acquired a special technique for dealing with them. Marriott was a shrewd man, and he had a natural facility for getting on to good terms with his fellow beings, and for influencing them in the right direction. "The right direction," in Marriott's judgment, was generally synonymous with the welfare of Langston's—but then an author's prosperity was bound up with the prosperity of his publisher, so business and magnanimity could be happily combined in easing their association.

Since Langston's was a very prosperous firm, Marriott was an exceedingly busy man, but he knew that the best way of saving time sometimes was to appear prodigal of it, and when Michael Ashe came to see him, Marriott would dismiss his stenographer, push his writing pad away, and prepare for an hour's discursive gossip on matters bookish and academic. Ashe was a celebrity by now. Although his published novels only reached half a dozen, they were regarded as the best things of their type since Conrad,—and they sold! Dear me, how they did sell! A little paper slip, detailing sales for the past month, was tucked under the blotter on Marriott's table, and the geniality with which he listened to Ashe criticising some of his contemporaries was not a little inspired by those surprising figures on the hidden slip.

"The fact is, one gets stereotyped and then one slides down-hill," said Ashe. "Even Galsworthy did, for all his felicity of manner and his power of delineating character. His later work wasn't as good as his middle period. I'm thinking of breaking fresh ground in my next book; I'm getting stylised, and that's the onset of fossilisation via coagulation. I'm going to run amok, and take to crime for a living."

"My dear Ashe!" Marriott's tone was scandalised, for all that he had understood the other's trend of thought perfectly. "If you're afraid of getting stale,—and I for one, don't see any signs of it—go for a voyage. Get a passage to Australia or Tristan da Cunha or Tierra,—in a wind-jammer for preference, but don't utter these wild threats. Crime stories are a legitimate branch of fiction, but they're mere ephemerals,—selling like hot cakes today, and gone tomorrow."

"What about this one, most learned judge?" Ashe went to the bookcase and picked out one of the volumes,—all produced by the firm of Langston—that were packed there into such neat ranks.

"*The Charterhouse Case*, by Vivian Lestrange," he read. "Is that your notion of an ephemeral, oh worthy Daniel? Three years ago, wasn't it? and the sales still good, I take it?"

"Oh, very good, very good indeed," said Marriott. "That's a remarkable book,—have you read it?"

"Yes, I've read it," replied Ashe, "and re-read it. I picked it up by chance in a hotel lounge in Juan les Pins, and since then I've read everything the beggar's written. He's a damn fine writer, and it doesn't matter in his case if it's a crime or belles-lettres. He can write, as only one man in a million can write. That book's a work of art, from whatever point you view it. He's achieved the impossible,—or at least the improbable—by writing a crime story that is in the rank of first rate novels. His writing, his characterisation, and his situations all disarm criticism."

"Yes, yes," put in Marriott. "I'll grant you that Vivian Lestrange is unique, but if you allow yourself to be influenced into taking up his line because you admire the way he does it—"

"Well! Well! Well! To think that I've lived to be accused of wishing to plagiarise," interpolated Ashe. "I'm only condemning you out of your own mouth! But tell me this. Am I right in guessing that Vivian Lestrange is merely a nom-de-guerre covering the excursions of a well-known writer?"

"No, no. You're wrong there," said Marriott. "Lestrange is a recluse, and I'm bound to respect his wish for seclusion. As you may have noticed, there are no facts to be gathered about him in such publications as the *Authors' Year Book*, neither has any photographer induced him to sit for his portrait,—but I shan't be breaking any confidences when I tell you that I believe *The Charterhouse Case* was Lestrange's first novel."

"Odd," mused Ashe. "It seems too mature, and yet too easy, to be a first book. It was an original idea of course, to start with the trial and sentence, go on with life in prison, and then make your condemned felon turn detective when he's released, and achieve the balance by committing the very crime of which he was wrongly accused. You know, I think that description of a convict's life on Dartmoor is one of the most remarkable things I've ever read. I couldn't help asking myself how the dickens Lestrange got his facts and local colour. One's left with the impression that he must have served time himself."

Marriott laughed,—a real hearty laugh full of genuine amusement, with nothing forced about it.

"I'm almost sorry to disillusion you, my dear fellow," he said, when he had managed to subdue his mirth, "but I can assure you that you're very wide of the mark. That description of Dartmoor was the product of a remarkable imagination, and of much study of reports on prison conditions and reforms,—as kindly provided by H.M.'s Stationery Office."

Seeing that Ashe was looking a bit nettled, Marriott hastened to change his tone. It was a mistake to have laughed at the writer's suggestion,—one ought to have made him laugh first, and then have joined in.

"As a matter of fact," he went on gravely, "we all take that description of prison life at its face value. It's very well written, and there's feeling in it, and how can we say from our own experience, 'No. That's not accurate. That didn't happen?' We've never been 'inside.' Consequently we can only judge those chapters from the point of view of craftmanship and reasonable probability. As you so justly observed," and Marriott waved a courtly hand, "the craftmanship of Lestrange is beyond criticism."

Michael Ashe seemed a little mollified by the other's change of front, and nodded his head in agreement.

"Yes, I see your point," he said. "Just as in these stories of Scotland Yard detectives, we take a great deal for granted as long as our sense of credibility isn't outraged. I don't expect the average writer of a thriller knows anything more about the Yard than I do,—that it's a place where one hopes to find one's lost umbrella,—only one never does."

Marriott chuckled;—"Quite, quite," he murmured, "though to do them justice, some of the 'thriller merchants' take an infinite amount of trouble to get their facts vetted. The standard is going up steadily…"

"Yes, I daresay," said Ashe interrupting not too politely, "but getting back to our original subject—I'm interested in this man Lestrange, only, owing to what you call his 'reclusiveness' or 'exclusiveness,' one doesn't meet him in the ordinary way. Look here, Marriott. Can't you arrange a dinner and introduce us to one another? I'm taking it for granted that the chap isn't a freak, or a pathological curiosity…"

"Nothing of that kind, nothing at all," interpolated Marriott quickly. "Vivian Lestrange struck me as being a very normal, likeable, healthy individual. But as to your suggestion about the dinner party, of course I can't do more than put it to Lestrange…"

"Oh, obviously, it's up to him," replied Ashe. "I'm not wanting to force myself on him, but you might say that I should very much like to meet him, and if he dislikes being talked about, I'm quite capable of respecting that idiosyncrasy."

"Leave it to me, my dear fellow," said Marriott genially. "If the meeting isn't arranged I assure you it won't be for lack of effort on my part… Now about this limited edition."

For the next few minutes they discussed "high finance,"—royalties, serial rights, cheap editions and the like,—subjects dear to the hearts of both, and at last Ashe got up to go. His final remark was, "See what you can do about Lestrange. I'm really keen to meet him."

When he had gone, a little smile of amusement flickered across Marriott's face, and he drew his telephone towards him, and plugged in the connection which put him through to the office of his colleague,—Robert Bailey. The latter was responsible for the publicity and sales departments, whereas Marriott dealt with authors' contracts, readers and so forth.

"Hullo. Ashe gone yet?" enquired Bailey, when he heard Andrew Marriott's deep voice.

"Yes. He's just left. What do you think he's got into his head now? He wants to meet Vivian Lestrange."

"Well, I'm…" exclaimed Bailey. "What the deuce put that into his head?… And what the dickens did you tell him?…"

"I told him I'd pass his message on to Lestrange, and left it at that. You know I've been thinking for sometime past that this secrecy business is a bit tiresome. People are making the most absurd suggestions. Ashe had actually got a bee in his bonnet that Vivian Lestrange is an ex-convict,—besides the Press isn't pleased about it."

"It's all a bit difficult, I grant you," said Bailey thoughtfully, "but we can't blow the gaff without permission."

"No, no! of course not! I wasn't even contemplating such a step," protested Marriott, "but I do think I'll write and put in a suggestion about a little dinner just for the four of us. Ashe is a quite trustworthy fellow, and he'll give nothing away, but if he were in a position to say that he'd actually *met* Lestrange,—drop a word to the P.E.N. for instance, it would be an excellent thing. Besides, Ashe is a very attractive personality, and he's much in the public eye these days. At any rate, there'd be no harm in seeing how the suggestion is taken."

"Well, I leave it to you," replied Bailey. "But I don't think the party will materialise."

"We shall see," said Marriott, and rang off. Leaning back in his chair, Marriott gave himself up to amused reminiscence. When Langston's had published *The Charterhouse Case*,—and it had been the biggest success of the publishing year,—Marriott had invited the author to come and dine with him. Lestrange had replied in a courteous little letter, declining the invitation on the grounds that he was a semi-invalid who seldom went beyond his own garden. He had also written that personal publicity of any kind was very distasteful to him, that the public need only know an author through the medium of his work. The situation had remained the same for nearly three years, during which Lestrange's reputation had steadily increased, though the public learned nothing of the author. Then, some six months ago, a situation developed which called for a personal interview. A certain passage in Lestrange's new novel—then at the printer's—had caused Marriott to wrinkle his brows in consternation. Of course, as the reader pointed out, it was a matter of interpretation, but one never knew with the public, and reviewers were an incalculable lot. Langston's wouldn't like to have any mud thrown—and then there were the libraries…

Marriott had nodded his wise head, and had written to Vivian Lestrange a very tactful letter, explaining the difficulty and begging that he might be allowed to come and talk the matter over. Lestrange, in reply, said he would call on Marriott, and discuss the difficulty on condition that the publishers would give an undertaking to respect his anonymity and give no hint of his real personality to anybody.

Much intrigued, Marriott had given the undertaking asked for, and had looked forward with a lively interest to meeting the writer whose fame was known in three continents.

On the morning of the appointment, Marriott's clerk brought him a letter marked "Urgent and personal." Opening it he found a visiting card:

VIVIAN LESTRANGE
Temple Grove,
Hampstead.

"Ask the gentleman to come in," said Marriot to the messenger who had brought the letter. The young man goggled at him.

"Please, sir," he began, but was cut short.

"At once," said Marriott firmly.

Expecting he knew not what,—from the Prime Minister to the Prince of Wales, Marriott watched the door with the keenest curiosity he had ever felt,—and then he had the surprise of his life when a tall, slim young woman entered the room, and held out her hand, a smile in her eyes as she looked at him.

"I'm afraid this is a shock for you, Mr. Marriott," she said calmly, "but it's your fault really. I never said I was a man. I merely refrained from contradicting your original assumption."

Marriott began to laugh,—he really couldn't help it, and Vivian Lestrange laughed too, and their laughter melted away any strangeness from their first meeting.

"God bless my soul!" exclaimed the publisher. "To think I have been flattering myself for years that I could tell a man's writing from a woman's…"

"Well, it's jolly good for you to know you can't," she replied laughingly. "I get so sick of that theory. The minute a reviewer learns from some gossip that so and so is a woman, he promptly writes 'there is a touch of femininity about the writings of X.Y.Z. Her descriptions are above criticism, but her dialogue betrays her sex.' It's all my eye and Betty Martin!"

Once again Marriott laughed. "My dear young lady, you are the exception to prove the rule."

"That is merely an admission of defeat," retorted Vivian
Lestrange. "You have met your Waterloo, and incidentally I'm
not very young, and far from ladylike in some respects, as you
may have observed from my books. Now let's get down to it. I
agree with you that this passage could do with some remodelling.
I wasn't hinting at perversion when I wrote it. That is a subject
which isn't in my line at all."

Sitting opposite to the publisher, she produced a sheet of
notes from her bag, and began to suggest alternative versions
for the offending passage. As she talked, Marriott was more and
more impressed by her shrewdness, and the clear-mindedness
which characterised everything she said. She was a very per-
sonable young woman, this Vivian Lestrange, tall and slim,
yet broad-shouldered, in build somewhat boyish. Her fair hair
which gleamed smoothly under the small blue hat, was close
cropped, leaving her ears uncovered. Her skin was admirable,
fresh and healthy, with only a slight suggestion of make up, and
the grey-blue eyes which studied Marriott so steadily looked
straight into his own with an impersonal deliberation. She was
dressed in a well cut navy-blue suit, with a light blue shirt and
dark tie. Studying her more closely, Marriott assessed her age at
something over thirty,—the slim figure and fresh skin had given
a first impression of youthfulness, but as she talked, she gave
evidence of a mature and thoughtful mind.

Having dealt with the difficulty which had been the cause
of her visit, she went on to sketch the outlines of the novel on
which she was now engaged. Sitting sideways to Marriott, her
chair pushed back from the table, her feet crossed and her eyes
studying the etchings on the further wall, she talked in a low
clear voice, singularly deliberate in diction. Marriott, studying

her regular profile, decided that the voice and the face were well matched, both admirable, but queerly lacking in feeling,— as dispassionate as the mind of a mathematician. When he expressed enthusiasm over the ideas she was sketching out for his benefit, Vivian Lestrange smiled at him very pleasantly, but yet conveyed the impression that it was her own judgment that mattered, nothing else.

"Upon my soul, the coolest creature I ever met in my life!" exclaimed Andrew Marriott, when describing the interview to Bailley. "Good brains, good looks, good breeding, and yet as remote as a stone carving. One couldn't get to grips with her, every time I put in a friendly word, she just smiled through me!"

Remembering his first interview with Vivian Lestrange after Ashe had left him, Marriott chuckled to himself. What would Ashe make of her, he asked himself?—Ashe who was adored by every woman he met, and who took adoration as his due? Reaching out for a sheet of note-paper, Marriott began to write a letter,—a very rare occurrence for one to whom dictation was second nature.

"My dear Miss Lestrange," he wrote. "I have just been having a talk with Michael Ashe. Some time ago you expressed admiration of his work, and this morning he was telling me how greatly he admired yours. (A feather in your cap, for he is a carping critic.) He continued by saying he wanted to meet Lestrange, and asked me to tell him so.

"It is hardly necessary for me to add that Ashe gained no notions of your identity from me, but I said that I would pass on his suggestion for a meeting to you.

"I think,—in fact I am certain—that you would find Ashe an interesting personality. He is also one of those who can keep a secret, and you need have no fear that he would endanger yours. If I were not positive about this I would not suggest the meeting, but I have had a large experience of human nature, and experience is a wise guide.

"If the idea commends itself to you, will you do me the honour of dining with me and my colleague, Mr. Bailley, to meet Mr. Ashe? It would give us all very great pleasure, and as you know, we will ensure that our party shall not endanger your secret.

"With kindest regards,
"Believe me, sincerely yours,
"ANDREW MARRIOTT."

Bailley smiled sceptically when Marriott told him of his letter.

"You're an optimist," he said to his colleague. "You want to persuade Vivian Lestrange to come out of her shell, and you're dangling Michael Ashe as a bait. It won't work, my lad, it won't work."

Marriott did not believe that it would work himself, but he had just a vague hope at the back of his mind. Vivian Lestrange had once shown a very definite interest when she had spoken of Michael Ashe,—something more personal than the cool detachment which characterised her attitude towards most subjects. As Marriott knew, there are hardly any writers in the world who do not enjoy appreciation of their work from someone whom they themselves admire.

He had not long to wait. The next morning came a letter answering his own.

"Dear Mr. Marriott,

"Many thanks for your letter. It will give me much pleasure to dine with you and Mr. Bailley, and to meet Mr. Ashe. Any evening next week would suit me.

"Of course I accept your assurances that Mr. Ashe will respect my secret as you have done.

"Sincerely yours,
"VIVIAN LESTRANGE."

Marriott showed the letter to Bailley with a chuckle.

"Human after all," he observed. "I really feel quite consoled. All my theories about women were being destroyed,—frozen out by the icy detachment of that remarkable young woman. Now I must get hold of Ashe and tell him he can have his wish if he will pledge himself to respect a fellow author's fancies."

CHAPTER II

O N THE EVENING ARRANGED FOR HIS DINNER PARTY, Andrew Marriott fussed around his beautiful Bloomsbury flat until his housekeeper, Mrs. Edge, got positively annoyed.

"Anybody'd think he'd got the King and the Queen and the Prince of Wales all coming together," she confided to her husband. Mrs. Edge was a very good cook and a very capable manager, and her husband filled the roles of valet, butler and houseman as admirably as his wife did the cooking. "Queer ideas on parties some folks has," she went on. "Now a gentlemen's party's one thing, but if you're going to have mixed company, I do like to see it even. Sounds odd to me, that it do."

Michael Ashe arrived in good time for once, and gave a sardonic glance around the drawing-room. (Marriott was a bachelor, but he had a very pretty drawing-room.) Nodding to the two publishers, Ashe enquired,

"Well, which of you is it?" and Bailley laughed, with a twitch of his arched eyebrows.

"Not guilty, my boy, not guilty," he replied. "Try one of Marriott's cocktails. It'll help to steady your nerves for the coming fray…"

Vivian Lestrange was punctual too; just as Ashe had taken the glass proffered to him, the butler opened the door and announced "Miss Strange." Hastening across the room with outstretched hand, smiles wreathing his face, Marriott exclaimed:

"My dear Miss Lestrange! This is an honour for us all, and a long-hoped-for pleasure. May I introduce a fellow writer to you, Mr. Michael Ashe—Miss Vivian Lestrange."

There was a moment of utter silence; Ashe was so completely taken aback that he stood, his glass still in his hand, his lips parted, as tongue-tied as a schoolboy. Staring at the self-possessed woman in front of him, meeting her smiling, slightly mocking glance, he stammered incredulously,

"It's… it's impossible."

Turning to Marriott with a little shrug and a lift of her fair arched eyebrows, Vivian Lestrange murmured,

"Not Michael Ashe!… not *the* Michael Ashe! It's… it's impossible!"

The light mocking tone of her voice and the whole aplomb of her manner were so excellently calculated, that Marriott and Bailley laughed wholeheartedly, and Ashe, his face flushing, suddenly realised his boorishness.

"Miss Lestrange, I apologise wholeheartedly—I grovel. That was inexcusable of me, it was simply execrable!"

"It was," she replied coolly, her eyes mocking him. "Both inexcusable and execrable! And why, pray, that word impossible? Am I then so impossible? I live and learn."

Marriott could almost have applauded. Her voice was so delicious, her whole appearance, from her fair boyish head to the tips of her silver slippers, so completely admirable, that she had the man before her at such disadvantage as he might never have experienced before.

"You humiliate me!" protested Ashe, and his voice told of recovered poise. "Like the psalmist I am become a worm, and no man… but the worm turns when cornered! I said 'impossible,' and in that one word, under stress of feeling, gave voice to the conviction within me,—that no woman could have written *The Charterhouse Case*."

"'Murdering impossibility, to make what cannot be, slight work,'" she quoted in retort, taking the chair which Bailley was holding for her, and declining the cocktail which Marriott proffered, with an airy wave of her hand. "There is a proverb concerning a woman scorned," she went on, addressing her remark to the ceiling, with uptilted chin and smiling lips. "There might well be another about a man mistaken. 'Lay not thy hand upon the exclusiveness of man's conceit,' runneth the unwritten book of our modern Job, 'lest his integrity fail him in his rancour.'"

"No, not conceit," protested Ashe, leaning forward with a smile on his thin, handsome face, and Marriott and Bailley stood by, as it were, to watch the battle of words between Langston's two most famous lions. Vivian Lestrange believed in driving her advantage home, and she pounced before Ashe could formulate another word.

"Like the devil on another occasion, you quoted Holy Writ," she went on, "and I follow your example. 'I will demand of thee and answer thou me!' What but male conceit formulated that judgment of yours that no woman could have written a book which you admired? Is your estimate of all women the same? Were your mother, your sisters, your aunts, all congenital defectives? Were your female cousins half wits, and was your grandmother a moron?"

Laughter overcame the three men. Despite the energy of her words, the charm and gaiety of her voice saved them from any hint of acerbity, and Ashe raised his hands in token of defeat.

"Armistice, Kamerad, armistice!" he cried. "I will answer thee—out of the whirlwind! My mother, my non-existent sisters, my aunts and female cousins were of invulnerable intelligence,— 'of unmatched wit and judgment'—but none of them, oh most redoubtable debater, could have written ten consecutive pages without betraying their sex, in their choice of words, in their delineation of character, in their ethical judgments. Women have certain admirable qualities which men lack, but their qualities are characteristic of themselves."

"I often wonder what is at the root of that strange conviction which differentiates a woman's mind from a man's," replied Vivian Lestrange. "If I create a character in a novel, I consider the dual influences of environment and heredity. All my characters are derived from two parents,—a father and a mother, and their make up is influenced by both. For myself, I know that I resemble a father,—whom I cannot even remember,—in looks, in likes and dislikes, in my manner of thinking. This being so, how can it be reasonable to suppose that I should write in a style purely feminine, showing a mind solely derived from my mother,—whom I resemble hardly at all? I take it for granted," she added sweetly, "that you admit the validity of my original premise,—that each human being is derived from two parents, and that their mental equipment may resemble that of either father or mother?"

Ashe laughed again. "That is indubitable," he replied, "but your minds are not only influenced by heredity. Environment counts a lot. A woman sees only a limited amount of a man's point of view, and she can—as a rule—interpret only a limited portion of a man's mind."

"Surely your outlook is pure Victorianism," protested Vivian smilingly, "what you need is a course in biology. You envisage women still as the sheltered, emotional playthings of men. The woman of today is beginning to see through the fraud; in short, we are realising ourselves, developing our dual heritage from father and mother alike, and adumbrating the time when artistic creativeness,—genius even—may be expected from women and men alike. We are still handicapped by the habit of thought of centuries, still too prone to acknowledge the unique splendour of the gifted male,—but your 'weaker vessel' theory,—I deride it! I challenge it! In short, I deny it utterly and without reserve!"

That evening stood out in Marriott's mind for years as one of the most entertaining he had ever spent. Vivian Lestrange had too much *savoir faire*,—and too much inherent courtesy—to monopolise the conversation for long. Having expounded her original theme, she drew Marriott and Bailley into the conversational give and take, and she had the gift of making other people talk well. She tossed the ball hither and thither with a quickness of wit which was in itself delightful, and which displayed the epigrammatic qualities of a lively and cultivated mind. Only to Ashe, did she express the challenging mockery which had shown so well in the conversation before dinner, and more than once she had him floundering in a discussion, pouncing upon a too-sweeping generalisation, or an inexactitude in his facts.

Looking at his unconventional little party seated at the dinner table, Marriott thought that here was material for the novelist in the personalities of these two writers alone. Vivian Lestrange was dressed in the simplest of black georgette frocks, which fitted her slender body like a bud sheath. Her arms and shoulders were victoriously white, and her golden head so well shaped, that Marriott—who hated 'mannish' women—had to admit that the boyish crop became her. She wore long earrings of deep blue

lapis lazuli, and a necklace of the same stones around the base
of her rounded throat; her lips were reddened to just the degree
compatible with artistry, and her skin smoothly powdered so
that it had a damask quality.

Michael Ashe was a big fellow, with tanned face and slightly
grizzled fair hair. He had the long head and large bones of a
Norseman, and his blue eyes sometimes surveyed the young
woman opposite to him with a boldness that might have been
resented by any woman less cool and self-contained than the
plain-spoken object of it.

Marriott felt a few qualms at one period, as though he had
been playing with forces which he was unable to control. Ashe
was no Puritan, and Vivian Lestrange was provocative enough to
challenge the devil in him. Yet Marriott took comfort from the
very coolness of the young woman. Here was no inexperienced
girl to lose her head over a dominating man; remembering the
phrase she had used during their first meeting, Marriott chuckled
to himself. "Ashe has met his Waterloo. It'll be amusing to see
how he takes it."

When Vivian Lestrange rose to go,—shortly after eleven
o'clock, Ashe asked if he might drive her home, but she refused
his offer with characteristic directness, and asked for a taxi. As
she said good night to him she added,

"You have been entrusted with a secret tonight, because
Mr. Marriott,—who is my very dear friend—answered for your
integrity. If at any time, I hear a rumour that Vivian Lestrange
is a woman, I shall know whence that rumour came, and I shall
say two words,—'Male conceit.' We know that no woman can
keep a secret, for men have told us so. Look to your laurels, oh
man of integrity!"

"You can trust me, in this!" said Ashe, his blue eyes very bright and smiling, "but this dismissal is altogether too uncompromising. When do we meet again?"

"Who knows?" she laughed. "I am a recluse,—as Mr. Marriott will have told you. I came out this evening to meet Michael Ashe. As the Quakers say, 'I had a concern to know him.' I have enjoyed this evening, but I am going home again to think. Despite the adage about women's intuition, I base my behaviour on considered judgments. For the moment, good-bye."

She thanked Andrew Marriott very prettily for his hospitality, and held old Bailley's hand in her own with a warmth that made Ashe's sullen blue eyes flicker beneath their shaggy brows: her exit had all the cool finished grace which made her every action charming, and a curious flatness seemed to fall on the three men after she had left.

Marriott offered Ashe another whisky and soda, saying:

"Well. Now you know."

"Know what?" demanded Ashe. "That young woman would take the devil of a lot of knowing. I'm left guessing."

"A charming personality!" put in Bailley. "Damn it! one of the most delightful women I've ever met. She can be as feminist as she likes in theory, provided she's as attractive as that in practice. It's a pity she's so obstinate about hiding herself; that girl would take literary London by storm."

"Girl indeed!" retorted Ashe. "Not much girlish about that…"

Seeing Marriott's expression, he broke off and then continued less aggressively.

"Vivian Lestrange wants to have everything her own way; she claims intellectual equality with men while seeing to it that she maintains her privileges as a woman. If I had taken her at her own valuation and talked to her regardless of her sex, I should have stripped her pretensions naked. She hedges herself about with the bars of polite conventions, and then bleats about sex equality. God!"

Bailley uttered a little deprecating cough.

"My dear fellow, Miss Lestrange held a brief for one sort of equality only,—intellectual equality. She denied that it was possible to tell a woman's writing from a man's,—and her point was proved by her own work before you ever heard her put the argument into words. Further than that, she made no attempt to urge the matter. Moreover, she stressed the fact that it was only under modern conditions of civilisation that that equality could emerge. It's no use applying the criteria of the stone age to this discussion. We are a civilised community..."

"You're a damned old fool, Bailley!" said Ashe cheerfully. "You may be civilised. I'm not. Intelligence and civilisation aren't synonymous. Well, thanks very much for a very interesting and instructive evening. Like the lady in the case, I'm going home to think."

When Ashe also had taken his departure, Marriott rumpled up his grey hair in some perplexity.

"An interesting and instructive evening, certainly," he began and Bailley put in,

"But you're not over happy in your mind about it? Neither am I."

Marriott did not deny this. "He doesn't know where she lives," he observed, "and I fail to see how he's going to find out... I don't think he'll gossip, he has too much regard for his own reputation as a keeper of secrets."

Bailley began to chuckle, and then throwing back his head he laughed till he shook.

"Male conceit!" he ejaculated between spasms of mirth. "Male conceit! The impertinence of the hussy!"

The other's laughter was infectious, and Marriott began to chuckle too, but more restrainedly.

"It's as natural to assume conceit in an individual as to assume a centre to a circle," he pronounced, and Bailley gave him a dig in the ribs.

"Anatole France originated that," he commented, "not you, my boy. Another spot, Andrew. We'll drink to 'male conceit'!"

CHAPTER III

I T WAS ON A MONDAY EVENING, SOME THREE MONTHS AFTER Andrew Marriott's dinner party, that a young woman walked into Hampstead Police Station and asked to see the officer in charge. Sergeant Lumsden,—stout, observant, and polite,— smiled down on her benevolently.

"The Inspector's busy, Miss. Anything I can do for you?"

"Not unless you'd like to help me in a job of housebreaking," replied the visitor. "You see, Sergeant, the trouble isn't all my own, it's rather a confidential sort of trouble, and I don't want to go dropping bricks."

"Quite so, missy," replied the rather mystified, but still benevolent, sergeant. "Nasty things to drop, bricks. Now if you'd give me some idea of the trouble, so as to let the Inspector judge the importance of it for himself as it were? Is it what you'd call a criminal matter, or just a nuisance?"

"Well, it's certainly a nuisance,—in fact a damned nuisance," replied the lady, "also it may be a crime. Tell the Inspector that a respectable woman wants to see him about a matter of suspected murder or kidnapping,—a disappearance in other words. Here's my card, and tell him I'm perfectly *compos mentis*."

The sergeant gasped a little. "Look here, Miss. Our Inspector's not the sort what likes practical jokes."

"Neither do I. In fact I hate them," was the retort. "Tell him that, too, if you like."

Something in her voice, despite her nonchalant bearing, made the sergeant take in the card to his superior officer, and a few moments later the visitor was seated on a hard chair in a very bare office, facing a competent looking man in uniform, whose expression was more severe than benevolent.

"Yes, madam?" he enquired.

His visitor took a deep breath, as one about to plunge.

"My name is Eleanor Clarke, and I am secretary to Vivian Lestrange who lives at Temple Grove. I have come here because I can't get any answer at my employer's house, and I'm afraid something serious must have happened to him."

"Why do you suppose that?" asked the Inspector sceptically. The woman facing him had clasped her ungloved hands in her lap, and Inspector Bond noticed that her knuckles showed white, so tightly were her hands clenched together.

"Mr. Lestrange is rather eccentric, and he never goes out anywhere," she said. "His house is run by a woman named Mrs. Fife, who comes each morning at eight o'clock and stays until eight in the evening. I go to the house at ten o'clock every morning. This morning I went as usual, but I could not get any answer when I rang and knocked. I went for a walk and came back in half an hour's time, and could still get no answer. Then I noticed that the morning's milk had not been taken in, and the butcher boy, who came up while I was there, said he could get no answer, either. Then I decided to go and see Mrs. Fife. She had given me her address as 28 Canterbury Villas. When I got there I found no one had ever heard of her."

"I expect you made a mistake about the number," said the Inspector, but she shook her head and produced a slip of paper from her bag.

"No," she replied. "I made her write it down. It's quite clear."

The Inspector studied his visitor thoughtfully.

"Very well, Miss Clarke. You say that you made this discovery this morning; it is now six o'clock. Why did you not report the circumstances earlier if you felt they called for investigation?"

"Because I didn't want to make a fool of myself," retorted the other with some heat. "My employer is eccentric. He is a recluse, he never goes out, and he never receives visitors. He is a writer and he has a horror of publicity. No one knows who he is. You could ask every journalist in London about Vivian Lestrange—they would all know his name, but none of them have ever seen him, neither do they know anything about him. They'd give their ears—every man Jack of them—to know who he is. Now can you understand why I spent the day wandering about in a perfect turmoil of fear and indecision? If I came to you, I gave away my employer's secret which I am pledged to respect. Whatever I did, whatever plan I made, seemed to lead me into a worse mess. I came here at last because I had to do something,—and because I've always believed that the English police are fair and considerate. I had to tell somebody, and of all the alternatives I considered, the police seemed the least bad."

Bond could not help smiling, but his smile was quickly suppressed.

"Considering that you are practically an inmate of the house, didn't you consider that you would be justified in trying to force an entry?" he enquired, and she almost cried out at him:

"Oh, don't be silly! I'd have done anything,—or smashed anything,—to get inside, but it's impossible. There's a ten foot wall round three sides of the garden with revolving spikes on top of it. The fourth side is closed in by the blank wall of Lee-Vernon's studio. If I'd gone to a builder and told him to bring ladders to help me climb the wall, the story would have been all over Hampstead in half an hour,—and Mr. Lestrange's secret with it. He wouldn't let any of the tradesmen come inside the gate, they'd never seen him, and they don't know he exists. Mrs. Fife and I do all the ordering and pay all the bills."

The Inspector still regarded her critically. "Your employer gave you no hint that he might be going away?"

"The man thinks I'm an idiot," groaned Eleanor Clarke, and it was obvious that she did not refer to her employer. "Do you think I should have come to you with a yarn like this in order to get the sack from a very good job? Can't you realise that Mr. Lestrange was in the middle of a book, that we worked hard all Saturday and that he was crazy to get on with it? I'm his amanuensis,—I do all the writing and the typing. His hands are all stiff with rheumatism. Going away! Powers above! I shall burst in a minute!"

"You forget that I'm not a clairvoyant," said Bond calmly. "I can realise just as many facts as you choose to tell me, but it's not my business to anticipate them. Taking into consideration the evidence you have given, I will see that the matter is investigated. I should like the names of Mr. Lestrange's next of kin, if you know them?"

Eleanor Clarke sighed.

"And so should I,—and so would Fleet Street, and so would Langston's, and so *ad infinitum*!" she retorted. "He has no kin. I can't give you the name of a soul who knows him, because nobody does. No one ever comes to see him, and I've never written a personal letter for him all the time I've known him,—and that's three years."

"This is a very strange story," said Bond.

"It is," she replied, "in fact it's a Lestrange story! Here's another item of information for you. If you ring up Fleet Street and tell them what I've told you, you'll be in a position to retire on your winnings. Vivian Lestrange is NEWS!—news with capital letters and Fleet Street pays for news…"

"We are not in the habit of ringing up Fleet Street to augment our pay," said Bond calmly, and she replied:

"I know you're not. That's why I came here. The story I've told you is the best compliment the Metropolitan Police have ever been paid."

Bond looked down his nose and did not acknowledge the politeness.

"I take it that you have already advised your employer's publishers?" he enquired, and Miss Clarke gave a deep sigh.

"It's no use doing that," she said. "Langston's know *me* as Vivian Lestrange. At his wish I have always deputised for him, because he had this queer complex about hiding himself. If either of Langston's managers were here they would identify *me* as Vivian Lestrange… Now can you see the sort of mess I'm in?" she burst out. "I've been wondering all day how I could best disappear, and each time I realised that I couldn't do it until I'd been inside the house to find out what had happened. Haven't you any imagination?" she pleaded. "Can't you realise that something horrible may have happened behind that wall?"

"My business is to deal with facts," replied Bond. "Will you kindly tell me this. How many people know that your employer, Mr. Vivian Lestrange, really exists?"

"I know it, Mrs. Fife knows it, and you know it," she replied. "Apart from us, I don't know anybody else who does. Oh, don't say you're not going to do anything! I shall scream in a minute! I have been working myself up all day to find the courage to come here, and now you're not going to believe me!"

Bond gave the least shrug of his broad shoulders.

"I have cast no aspersions on your veracity," he began, and Eleanor Clarke began to laugh.

"You're word perfect!" she exclaimed between gusts of laughter. "Never mind about the aspersions. Come and find out."

In reply, Bond took up his pen and deliberately began to make notes.

"Your name and address, please?" he demanded acidly. "Since the situation has already waited all day to be dealt with, a few moments more or less will not greatly affect it."

Realising that her nervous mockery was having the opposite of the effect she intended, Eleanor Clarke made an effort to reply in a more seemly manner. Bond's notes did not take long, and then he got up and reached for his uniform cap.

"I will ask you to accompany me to the house in a few moments," he said stiffly, and left her by herself in the dreary little office.

About a quarter of an hour later two cars drew up in the quiet little cul-de-sac where stood Temple Grove. The first was a light van, with a couple of ladders loaded into it; the second a closed car in which Inspector Bond and a constable accompanied Eleanor Clarke. Before he alighted, Bond turned to his visitor.

"You will kindly stay here for the moment," he said. "I will tell you when you are needed."

He got out and went to the door in the wall, knocked and rang, and then waited. Receiving no answer, he beckoned to the two men in the van, and they began to unload the ladders.

Eleanor Clarke sat still in the car, twisting her fingers together, her face white now, as she watched the men erect a ladder against the wall; then one of them mounted it and hauled up the other ladder, which he negotiated with some difficulty over the revolving spikes, and finally got it down on the other side of the wall. Then Bond climbed up, surmounted the spikes neatly, and descended on the other side, followed by Constable Hewitt.

Bond was a very efficient police officer. If pedantic of speech and apparently slow in taking decisions, he was neither as unobservant nor as unimaginative as Eleanor Clarke had judged him to be. He had watched her pretty closely, and he knew that her flippant speech was partly due to nerves, but he had already adjudged the whole story to be the result of nerves. He thought that this was a matter of hysteria, and that Miss Clarke's story would prove to be another of those cases—well known to the police—when an informant tells some mysterious narrative which proves to have no foundation in fact. Bond had read a little psychology, and knew something of the mental conditions which led to the loss of memory on the one hand, and claims to notoriety on the other. Consequently he climbed over the wall in a state of mind coldly sceptical, and looked around the pleasant little garden placidly enough, while the big constable followed him over the wall. Temple Grove was a comfortable little two-storied house, standing in its own garden and entirely concealed from the road. The house faced south, and at the end of the garden rose the blank studio wall which Eleanor Clarke had mentioned. It was covered with creepers and a fine wistaria tree, which had just broken into flower. One side of the garden was bounded by the road, and close clipped lime trees concealed it from the adjacent house on the other side.

By the time Constable Hewitt had joined him, Bond was staring at the french window which opened on to the lawn, and Hewitt, following the Inspector's glance, gave a grunt.

"Something in it?" he enquired, for the glass of the window was starred by radiating cracks, and a round black hole showed clearly in the evening light.

"May be. May be not," said Bond, and walked towards the house. The window, he found, was only pushed to; opening it he found himself in a long low room, furnished as a study. A kneehole desk stood at right angles to the window, on his right as he stood looking round; in the wall on his left was a fireplace with an electric "log fire," a big easy chair on either side of it. Facing the window was a typist's desk, with the typewriter neatly covered; bookshelves, well filled, covered most of the walls to half their height, and a few etchings hung on the creamy space above the bookcases. It was all perfectly neat and peaceful; the parquet floor was polished, the rugs in place, and there was no indication of the unusual, save in that broken window pane.

Bond, after a careful glance at the polished floor, walked across the room, pressed down a switch with his handkerchief in his hand, and looked round again. He told Hewitt to stay where he was, and then proceeded to look under the desk, behind the chairs, under a settle which stood against the wall and behind the portière across the door in the corner.

"Nothing here," he said curtly. "You can come in. Walk in my traces as closely as you can."

Hewitt had already observed one fact. The floor was polished so well that Bond's footsteps—dusty from the dry roads and garden paths—showed perfectly clearly on that immaculate surface, but other footmarks there were none.

Following Bond closely, he crossed the room and went out of the door in the corner, and the two men stood in a pleasant little hall, rather dark until Bond switched on the light. There was a carved black oak chest, a table holding a gong, and a couple of chairs. A man's top coat hung on a peg by the door and some sticks stood in a corner. Opening another door, Bond looked into a small dining-room, furnished with a square table, four chairs, sideboard and wagon. Pewter plates gleamed on the sideboard, and a row of tankards stood in front of them. A few blue and white plates hung on the plain grey walls, and wrought iron candelabras held electric candles on either side of the chimney space. Once again all was orderly and polished. The remaining rooms on the ground floor were a small sitting-room, furnished with what Hewitt called "just bits of things," comfortable enough, but with furniture that was mainly odds and ends, a good deal worn and showing little of the taste of the other rooms,—and a kitchen and scullery. These latter were comfortably fitted, well kept, and showed an abundance of crockery and plate.

Still silent, Bond went upstairs and examined the four rooms on the first floor. The first one he entered was above the study and was a comfortably furnished bedroom. A man's brushes lay on the dressing-table, with a few odds and ends of manicure things and a bottle of bay rum. Pyjamas lay neatly folded on the bed, and a man's dark blue dressing-gown hung on the door. There was a large wardrobe with several suits, and a chest of drawers held socks and shirts, underwear, ties, collars and all the impedimenta of a man's clothing. Bond examined the drawers critically but without enlightenment. Everything that one might have expected to see was there and nothing else.—Neatly treed shoes, slippers, suspenders, braces, studs, links and tie-pins. "No shaving tackle," murmured Hewitt, but toothbrush and washing things were all in order. Hurrying into the other rooms, Bond found that only one of them was furnished. This held a dressing-table, a divan and easy chair, wardrobe and washstand, but no bed. A powder pot and face cream stood on the dressing-table, together with brush and comb. The wardrobe held only a woman's cardigan, umbrella, rain coat and slippers. Towels hung neatly folded on the rails, and soap and nail brush lay in the soap dish. Two smaller rooms were completely empty, and the bathroom with its big polished geyser was as innocent looking as the rest.

"What do you make of it, sir?" enquired Hewitt eagerly, but Bond only shrugged his shoulders.

"Nothing," he said. "That hole in the window is the only thing that's unusual, and that could have been made with a small stone or a pop gun. Go out by the front door and tell Miss Clarke to come in. You can send the van men away with the ladders and stand by in the garden door yourself until I want you."

Hewitt let himself out as bidden, and found that a path of crazy paving led to a door in the wall against the road. There were bolts at the top and bottom of the door but they were undrawn. An unusually large letter-box, fastened by a padlock, hung on the door, and there was a little grille with a sliding panel for observing those who sought to gain admittance. Hewitt also noticed that this door was the only means of access to house and garden. Tradesmen leaving goods at the kitchen door on the further side of the house would have had to pass the front door to reach the back entrance.

Opening the door in the wall by means of the Yale knob, Hewitt saw Eleanor Clarke looking eagerly out of the car at him, her face white and large eyed. The constable was a kindly soul, and he forgot the Inspector's suspicions of his informant, as he looked at the troubled face below him.

"Seems all right inside, Miss," said Hewitt cheerfully. "The Inspector wants you to step in and have a word with him."

She jumped out of the car with a look of relief, and fairly ran down the little paved path and in at the open front door. Finding Bond in the hall she burst out:

"Then everything's all right? I've just made a fuss for nothing?"

"There's no sign of any disturbance in the house," replied Bond, "but why did you throw a stone through the study window?"

If he hoped to catch her out, he failed.

"I haven't thrown any stones through anything," she retorted, "and if you think I'm hysterical or a lunatic, you've guessed wrong. I'm as reasonable as you are. What do you mean by throwing stones?"

Bond preceded her into the study and stood aside so that she could see the starred pane of glass. She stood staring intently with frowning face and then turned to him.

"How was that glass broken? If you had broken in when you got here, there would be glass on the floor,—and the hole's not large enough…"

"It was like that when we arrived, and the french window was open," replied Bond. "Apart from that, everything in the house is in order, and we have discovered nothing and nobody."

She drew a deep breath. "Mr. Lestrange would not have gone away and left the window open," she said. "Something must have happened to him. I knew there was something wrong when I couldn't find Mrs. Fife."

Bond stood and rubbed his head thoughtfully.

"It's all a bit vague," he said. "That window is the only evidence that anything is amiss. There is nothing illegal in the fact of a man going away suddenly and shutting up his house."

"But no man would willingly leave his study window open when he went away," she said quietly. "If Mr. Lestrange wanted to go away, or to disappear quietly, he would have either told me he was going away, or dismissed me. He wouldn't have left me to go to the police because I was afraid something awful had happened."

"Probably not," agreed Bond. "Do you know if there was anything of value in the house,—anything which might have been an incentive to robbery with violence?"

She shook her head. "Not to my knowledge. Mr. Lestrange kept a certain amount of ready cash, but not a great deal. He banked at the Westminster Bank, and I think Mrs. Fife cashed his cheques for him."

Bond heard this with some satisfaction. Apparently there would be some corroboration at the Bank of Lestrange's existence, and the Inspector thawed a little.

"Perhaps you'd sit down and tell me all that you can about your employer," he said, "and then we can look round and see if you notice anything out of order. At present, as you can judge for yourself, we have no case against anybody. You were quite right in informing us if you thought there was anything suspicious, but we shall have to be very careful. It's all somewhat obscure at present."

She flashed a smile at him, as though in relief that he had admitted at last that she had behaved reasonably, and pulled off

her close fitting hat as she sat down at the typist's table, running
her fingers through her close cropped hair.

"If the circumstances of my job had been less queer, I
shouldn't have come to you," she said, "but everyone has a
right to think of themselves, and I am in a difficult position. At
Mr. Lestrange's request, I had passed myself off for him to his
publishers, and if anything awful had happened in here, and I
hadn't come to you, I should have been in an impossible position.
If I had not come to you immediately, I should never have dared
to come at all. You've only my word for anything."

"Yes," said Bond. "That's the position in a nutshell; and now
you'd better tell me everything you can. How did you come to
be employed here?"

"I answered an advertisement in the local paper three years
ago. An author who gave his name as Thomas Browne wanted
a competent typist and secretary. I applied for the job and was
asked to call here. When I arrived, Mrs. Fife showed me into this
room, and I saw Mr. Lestrange sitting at that desk. He was a fairly
big man, but thin and bent, with grizzled brownish hair and a
small beard. He had two sticks beside him, and he wore gloves
on both hands. His hands were stiff and awkward, like those of
a man half crippled with rheumatism. He had a pleasant voice
and nice eyes, and I liked him. He said that he was a writer, and
that he needed an amanuensis and typist. After testing my speed
at shorthand and asking a good many questions, he said that I
would suit him very well if I would promise not to discuss him
or his affairs with anybody. I was a bit terse over this, for I'm not
a gossip or scandal-monger, but he went on and told me that he
had a loathing for any sort of personal publicity, and the only
secretary who would be any good to him was one who was

capable of keeping her own counsel and not mentioning a word about her job to other people."

Bond studied her closely while she talked; he liked the quiet voice and the straightforward way in which she told her story, and he found himself getting interested.

"At first I put him down for a neurotic of sorts," she went on. "His insistence on anonymity seemed to me rather pathetic. I knew of no Thomas Browne in the literary world of today,—and I'm quite fairly well read. I thought he was probably a crank, some obscure scholar who over-estimated his importance in a world which gives little heed to serious writers. Anyway, I managed to reassure him as to my own trustworthiness, he wrote to the people whose names I gave as references, and I started work here a week later."

"You knew then that Thomas Browne was Vivian Lestrange, and vice-versa?" enquired Bond, but Eleanor Clarke shook her head vigorously.

"No. I didn't learn that for nearly a year. At first he employed me in quite trivial stuff,—short stories and articles. He dictated, and I took down in shorthand and then typed. Sometimes he gave me a completed manuscript to type; his handwriting was rather difficult to decipher, crabbed and awkward, but I managed it and soon got used to it. I realised, of course, that he wrote amazingly well, even his slightest things had distinction, but I didn't know who published them. I was kept pretty busy during the day, and as I don't read magazines I never came across any of the shorter stuff he got published. I think during all that time he was trying me out,—deciding whether I was to be trusted and if he wanted to keep me on permanently."

"And he decided that he did?" enquired Bond.

She nodded. "Yes. We got on very well together, and one day, about six months after I came here,—he gave me a pile of manuscript and said that it was part of a novel he was writing. It was extraordinarily interesting, especially as he wanted to discuss part of it and get a woman's point of view concerning the women he had written about. It was after the novel was finished that he told me his real name was Vivian Lestrange. All those months I had been calling him Mr. Browne. After that he seemed to trust me altogether; I typed all his correspondence with his publishers, discussed his contracts, and helped with his business generally. Also, as I told you, I went to Langston's— Mr. Lestrange's publishers—and pretended that I was he, quite successfully."

"But why did he want you to do that?" demanded Bond. "It put you in a very invidious position, and I'm surprised that you agreed to it."

She shrugged her shoulders. "It was all a bit difficult. Langston's were being rather fussy, and Mr. Lestrange was afraid one of them would come poking an unwanted nose in here. I can't explain his complex about concealing himself; it always seemed to me that he was a bit dotty on that one point. Anyway, he said that Langston's were worrying him, and that he'd get no peace until they knew who he was, and that I could be the perfect secretary and save him from being bothered. He was rather pathetic over it, and I'd got so much into the habit of saving him the hundred and one small bothers that beset a writer, that I took him at his word and played Vivian Lestrange for him as a sort of joke. I took it quite light-heartedly, and it wasn't until later that I came to the conclusion that I'd landed myself in a rather questionable position."

"Was there any special reason to account for your qualms over what had seemed a very good joke?" enquired Bond, but she replied,

"No, nothing. It was just that Mr. Marriott and Mr. Bailley—the directors of Langston's—had been very nice to me, and I realised they'd consider my behaviour pretty low down. Everything went on quite placidly here until this morning and then as I told you I got frightened."

"I'm trying to get your position quite clear," said Bond. "If you were worried why didn't you consult your people at home?"

"Because I haven't any people to consult," she replied. "I simply have not got a relation in the world, that I know of, neither have I any intimate friends. I have only lived in London since 1920, I was brought up in Australia. I lived with my mother until she died in 1930, and we didn't get to know many people as she was rather an invalid. When she died I went to a Secretarial School and I made a few friends there, but there was no one I cared much for. My mother's old lawyer was a very good friend to me when I first came to London, but he died over two years ago. I live in a small service flat in Finchley Road. There was no one to whom I could go for advice. I thought about it all day, and at last I decided it was the police or nothing. I came to you for my own peace of mind."

"Yes, yes," said Bond, "but you knew your employer was eccentric. Any man who could behave as he did over asking you to impersonate him must be regarded as odd, to say the least of it. Going away suddenly like this might just be considered another piece of eccentricity."

"It might," she said slowly, "but I don't believe it. I know he was odd,—nobody knows it so well as I do. He lived this queer hidden life, never seeing anybody, never showing himself. Nobody would behave like that if they weren't afraid of something. When I couldn't get any answer here this morning, and I couldn't find Mrs. Fife either, I was certain something was wrong. I felt it in my bones. Now I've seen that window I know I was right. Something has happened... If the tradespeople had told you this house had been shut up for a week, and that nobody had counter-ordered the milk and papers, wouldn't you have done what you've done this morning—broken in and searched? And wouldn't you have looked for me, and asked why I hadn't let you know?"

"Quite so," said Bond sedately. "I'm not suggesting that it wasn't natural for you to feel worried, but there are often quite natural explanations to mysterious sounding stories. Now I think it'd be a good thing for you to have a look round the house with me and tell me if you notice anything missing, or out of order, and then we'll make a few enquiries. I should like to get into touch with this Mrs. Fife, too."

"Yes," said Eleanor Clarke, rising to her feet, "and so would I. I don't know if you believe in hunches, Inspector, but I've got one now. No one will ever see Mrs. Fife or Mr. Lestrange again. They've just gone,—and left me guessing... Would you like to write me a testimonial, Inspector, as a hard working, sober and respectable secretary? You might omit the fact that my employers occasionally disappear in an unaccountable manner."

"I think that you are too fond of indulging your imagination, Miss Lestrange," said Bond coldly, and she fairly jumped.

"And you're too fond of guessing," she retorted, "and your guess is a rotten one, anyway."

CHAPTER IV

"THE FACT IS, I'M IN A CLEFT STICK, SIR," SAID INSPECTOR Bond ruefully.

It was a week after Eleanor Clarke had paid her visit to the police station, and Bond, who had done a steady week's work investigating the disappearance of Vivian Lestrange, had come to Scotland Yard to report his case and discuss the whole matter with Chief Inspector Warner of the Criminal Investigation Department. The latter was a tall, fair, well-built fellow, with a tanned face, and clear-cut profile;—just the type of man who might be seen mounted on a fine horse, directing the traffic at Hyde Park Corner, eliciting the comment that "these London cops are good lookers" from the ubiquitous American visitor. In mufti, Warner looked just as spruce and well groomed as he did when he wore a uniform coat; he was pleasant to look at because his appearance was clean and cool and competent, and his shrewd grey eyes were amused as he looked at Bond's crestfallen face.

"No, not a cleft stick," he answered. "The analogy's too static. You're on the horns of a dilemma, oscillating between the points, like a compass suffering interference. The evidence leads you to expect foul play,—of a nature not specified,—and your private judgment insists that the Force is having its leg pulled by a young woman with imagination and no principles. Say if you give me the main points of your investigation, and I'll tell you if I see a snag."

Bond settled to his tale.

"According to Miss Clarke's evidence, the household at Temple Grove consisted of three people,—her employer, Vivian Lestrange, who lived there, Mrs. Fife, the housekeeper, who came every day from eight in the morning until eight in the evening, and herself, who came at ten in the morning and left at five o'clock. Vivian Lestrange is described as a tall bearded man, age between fifty and sixty, a bit lame and very stiff, whose hands were slightly crippled with rheumatism, and who always wore gloves. That's Miss Clarke's description of him, but we can't find anybody else who has seen him; we have only her word for it that he existed—or exists. Mrs. Fife is undoubtedly real. She is known to the tradespeople as a dour competent woman of fifty, who knew her own mind, was a good shopper, and settled the household bills in cash every week. She is described as a stout, dark-haired woman of fifty, and the tradespeople in Heath Terrace gossiped about her a good bit because she never let any of the errand boys come inside the gate of Temple Grove. The only people who ever got inside the house—as far as I can make out—were the men who read the gas and electric meters, and while they did that Mrs. Fife stood over them like a dragon. The tradesmen's books were all in the name of Mr. Thomas Browne,—the name under which Miss Clarke's employer is said to have originally engaged her."

"It's an attractive story," murmured Warner. "I'm quite anxious to meet Miss Clarke. She sounds an original."

Bond grunted. "She's sharp enough," he said. "I don't know whether you will catch her out or not. I can't. Well, so much for Mrs. Fife. We can't find her anywhere, and nobody's volunteered a single scrap of useful information. The woman was there at

Temple Grove every day until last Saturday, and she was seen walking down Temple Place towards Heath Street on Saturday evening. After that, nothing."

"So much for the vanished personnel,—we'll deal with Miss Clarke later," said Warner serenely. "Now tell me about the house. It sounds rather a nice house,—just the sort of thing I've wanted for a long time."

Bond only looked irritable in reply to this sally; his chief weakness was a dislike of being laughed at, and he was not at his best over the case of Vivian Lestrange, because he felt that he was being made a fool of, and yet was unable to prove it.

"Temple Grove is a detached, two storey, non-basement house built in the 'eighties," he replied in his most official voice. "Here are plans which I have made of both floors. The study has been polished so well that we found no finger-prints on any of the furniture, nor yet on the door plates, or door handles, or windows. The floor appears to have been first scrubbed and then polished, and no one had walked across it since the polishing was done unless they wore clean list slippers which would not leave a mark. There is a large number of books in the room, but most of them appear to have been bought second-hand,—many from Foyle's and some from Hatchard's, and the finger-prints on them are many and various. The desk contained a quantity of manuscript and typescript, bills (all receipted), reference books and pamphlets, and the usual collection of pens and pencils. On the typescript and manuscript, the only finger-prints are Miss Clarke's."

"Yes," murmured Warner. "The problematical author wore gloves,—a thoughtful precaution that."

"Very," returned Bond dryly. "Anyhow, we found nothing in that room to prove that a bearded man named Lestrange had ever lived in it. There was, as I said, quantities of manuscript. The handwriting,—here is a specimen—is in a queer crabbed style."

He handed a paper to Warner who studied it for a moment.

"Left handed?" he queried.

"Undoubtedly," replied Bond. "The experts told us that, and Miss Clarke ratified their decision by telling us that her employer always wrote with his left hand. This"—handing another slip of paper—"is a specimen of Miss Clarke's own writing, left-handed and right-handed."

Warner's lips twitched a little as he studied the fresh exhibits. The one showed a very charming flowing writing, admirably legible, with each letter well formed and a consistent slope which made it pleasant to read. Very pretty writing, thought Warner, denoting character, with a sense of detail and picturesqueness, but essentially a woman's hand. The other sheet showed a round childish scrawl, in which an effort had been made to achieve the copy-book characters of early youth. The lines were uneven and sloped up and down in a manner that looked inebriated. "I can't write with my left hand," had scrawled Miss Clarke. "This scrawl is not an affectation but a genuine disability. I am trying, but I can't do any better than this."

Warner laughed a little. "If she were really pulling our legs she would be enjoying herself quite a lot," he observed. "Her normal handwriting indicates a sense of detail, and if you are right in your suspicions, she has foreseen most contingencies. What do the experts make of this?"

"Nothing at all," said Bond disgustedly, "but there's nothing in that. They say that there isn't a character in common between the Lestrange writing and Eleanor Clarke's, but commonsense tells you that anybody can teach themselves to write with their left hand, and anybody could produce an idiotic scrawl like that in the manner in which that one was produced. She wrote about one letter a minute and pretended that she couldn't control a pen with her left hand at all. Now watch…"

Producing a pencil and paper, Bond wrote his name and address with his left hand, carefully and painstakingly. He then wrote the same words with his right hand, and finally wrote them again with his left in an uncertain babyish scrawl resembling Eleanor Clarke's effort.

"I taught myself to write with my left hand a couple of years ago, when I had broken my right wrist," he said. "No expert could say that there was anything in common between my right-hand and left-hand writing, neither could they say that that baby's first effort had anything in common with the others. That's as plain as daylight."

"Quite," agreed Warner cheerfully. "You've proved to your own satisfaction that so far as handwriting goes, Miss Clarke could have produced the manuscript you found at Temple Grove. Also there was no proof of Mr. Lestrange's existence in the study. What about the bedroom. Swept and garnished?"

"Quite," said Bond, in Warner's manner, and the Chief Inspector grinned.

"Don't get embittered over it," he said mildly. "Personally, I'm prepared to enjoy working on this case. The young woman has wits, it seems."

"The bedroom contained all that it should, and nothing that it shouldn't," said Bond. "A man's kit all complete; suits pretty well worn, but recently dry cleaned; pants, vests, collars and all the rest, nicely laundered. Clean bedclothes not yet slept in, clean towels, too. No tailor's marks in anything, but the suits were all made by different firms,—two of them were bought ready made, and there's one that was probably bought in America. Any second-hand clothes agency like Peter Dean's in the Edgware Road could have supplied the lot. Similarly with shoes; they're all size nine and reasonably well worn."

"Do the suits, underclothes, collars and shoes seem consistent,—as though one man might have worn the lot?" enquired Warner, and Bond nodded.

"Oh, yes. If my suspicions are anywhere near the truth, I give the young woman full marks for attention to detail. There's nothing to bowl her out among those clothes, and I can tell you I've been through them pretty carefully. We've got Baines to try them on,—he's a fellow of five foot eleven, weighs eleven stone and is rather sparely built. The things fitted him all right, and the shoes as well. Nothing doing there."

"Now let me have your theory in detail," said Warner. "I can see your point,—that Vivian Lestrange and Eleanor Clarke are identical."

Bond leaned back in his chair. "I think she's abnormal," he said. "I believe she wrote those Lestrange books, and at first enjoyed being taken for a man, and was careful to conceal her identity. Then the fun began to pall, and she looked around for some other means of acquiring notoriety. It is quite reasonable psychology," he protested, as though Warner were arguing with him. "Psychologists will tell you that the notoriety complex is by no means unusual; it's just an aberration of an often original brain. The Clarke girl took the house (I'll tell you about that later), having got the housekeeper in, to be her accomplice, and laid the foundations of this double-life story, intending to exploit it for her own amusement later on. She taught herself to write with her left hand, opened a banking account as Vivian Lestrange and gradually got her evidence together. She bought the man's kit at a second-hand stores, and then, when she was ready, came and told her story to us and had the pleasure of watching us investigate.

"After all, I couldn't very well help myself," concluded Bond, his voice telling of the exasperation in his mind. "That study window was open, and there was a hole like a bullet hole through the glass. It might have been a crime,—it still may be…"

"Indeed it may," said Warner, and this time he did not smile. "You have made out a perfectly sensible case, Bond, and I appreciate your reasoning. I haven't had any contact with the case yet, but I'll give you my opinion for what it's worth. I don't believe those books by Vivian Lestrange were written by a woman, and it'll take a lot to make me change that opinion. Further, I can't imagine Vivian Lestrange seeking notoriety or advertisement; he's definitely not the type. His books are their own advertisement, the mind that created them was not a mind which appeals to the sensation monger. It's obvious that there's something odd about that household at Temple Grove. It's furtive, and I'm prepared to believe that something queer lies behind the whole story."

Warner smiled suddenly at the sceptical face across the table.

"We're both of us biased at the outset," he said, "and that's all wrong, but perhaps your bias and mine will correct each other's. Now I want you to go on and tell me all you've found out about the individual who leased Temple Grove,—House agents, bankers and all that."

Bond nodded. "Temple Grove was leased in 1925, from the owners, by a man named Rogerson," he said. "He took it on a ten years' agreement. In 1931 he had to go abroad, and wanted to let the place—semi-furnished—in a hurry. The agents who negotiated it—Blacks, of Baker Street—tell me that they were called on by Mrs. Fife who had instructions to view Temple Grove for her master, Mr. Lestrange, the latter being an invalid. They soon heard from Lestrange that the place was just what he wanted, and he asked for a year's lease, rent payable in advance, with an option at the end of the year, saying he might take over the remainder of the lease and buy the furniture at a valuation if the place suited him. He gave his bankers as reference.

"Since Rogerson was in a hurry to get things settled, he jumped at the offer, pocketed the year's rent and went abroad without even seeing his tenant. At the end of the year Lestrange took over the remainder of the lease, bought the furniture, and everybody was satisfied,—but no one ever saw him in person.

"As for Lestrange's bankers, he wrote them in 1930,—after *The Charterhouse Case* was published, saying he wished to open a current account, and giving his publisher's name. Once again the plea of invalidism enabled him to avoid a personal visit, and he has paid in his publisher's cheques ever since, maintaining a steady balance, and behaving admirably from the banker's point of view. He was in the habit of drawing out fairly large sums occasionally and was known to have had dealings with a firm of brokers named Rank, in Lombard Street.

"Last Saturday Mrs. Fife cashed (by arrangement) a cheque for £400, leaving only £50 in Lestrange's current account and nothing in deposit. At his request the money was paid in £1 notes. Needless to say there's no sign of it anywhere in the house."

"The notes were in sequence, I suppose?" asked Warner and Bond nodded. "The bank gave us the numbers, and they're being watched. So far nothing doing."

"Enquired at the Passport Office?" asked Warner, and Bond nodded.

"Yes. No Vivian Lestrange. Ten Thomas Brownes. None of them our man."

"You haven't let much slip," said Warner.

"I've done everything that I could think of," replied Bond, "and yet I'm no further forward than I was when that young woman walked into my office last week and told me her little story about her missing employer."

"By the way, you haven't told me what Langston's have got to say about it all," said Warner, and Bond shrugged his shoulders.

"They are about as helpful as everybody else," he said. "The two principals, Marriott and Bailley are oldish men; pleasant enough fellows in a bookish way and very competent at their own business, no doubt. They're simply out of their depths in this business, and say quite frankly that they don't know what to believe. When Lestrange's first manuscript was sent to them, they jumped at it, scenting a winner. They accepted it at once, and offered him a very decent contract involving an option on his next two books. They're a good firm and they treat their writers well. Of course they assumed Vivian Lestrange was a man, and all the correspondence was carried out on that assumption. Then last year Miss Eleanor Clarke goes and calls on them as cool as brass, and introduces herself as Vivian Lestrange,—"

"And they swallowed it?" put in Warner incredulously.

"They swallowed it all right. Vivian is a woman's name as well as a man's. She is an unusual person certainly, and can talk with a cool assurance that's very convincing. Anyway Langston's took her for granted. Now she says she's not Vivian Lestrange, and only played the part at her employer's wish. The publishers are pretty sick over it anyway. Nobody likes being fooled, and whatever happens they've been fooled handsomely. Marriott says 'You've got to find Vivian Lestrange for us, he's too valuable to lose.' It's the devil and all," concluded Bond despondently.

"It's got the merit of freshness, so far," said Warner. "I'm tired to death of confidence men and defaulting solicitors and homicidal maniacs; all this is a change from the trivial round and common task, and if it doesn't prove to be one of the most interesting cases we've ever handled, then I'm a Chinaman. Now tell me about your *bête noire*, the pseudo authoress with the winning manner."

Bond snorted. "You'd better have a talk with her; perhaps you'll like her better than I do. Here's her history.

"Born in 1900 in a farmhouse in the parish of Stanway, Gloucestershire. Her mother was named Elizabeth Clarke and the child was born out of wedlock. In 1902 the mother took her baby with her to Australia where they joined the father on a homestead near Ballarat. In 1910 the father died and the mother and daughter lived in Ballarat until early in 1914. They then returned to Europe—the mother saying that she had come into a legacy,—and they lived in Switzerland until 1920. Then they returned to England and took part of a house in the Finchley Road, near the old Eyre Arms Tavern. The house was demolished a few years ago when Eyre Court was built. In 1925 the mother died, and the daughter found herself very badly off. She trained as a Secretary at the Grosvenor Bureau and got odd office jobs until 1930, when according to her own account,

Vivian Lestrange employed her. She lives in a small service flat in that new block in Finchley Road. Now the odd part of her story is this. There's no one to corroborate most of it. When Mrs. Clarke and her daughter first came to live in England they had no friends except an elderly solicitor named Franks, who managed their affairs for them. He died in 1929, so he's no help to us. Apparently the mother and daughter were great friends and companions and they didn't bother about other people's company. Later the mother became invalidish and the girl gave all her time to looking after her. It wasn't until the mother's death that Eleanor Clarke learned that she was illegitimate, and that her mother's income died with her. Naturally, during the girl's secretarial training she made various friends, but she's one of those odd independent women who don't cotton on to their own sex. According to her own account, she hadn't any intimate friends, she's 'a pelican in the wilderness' to use her own expression. The more I consider her, the more I think she's likely to have invented the whole yarn," concluded Bond. "She's just one of those queer secretive women who might make a bid for notoriety. Lots of brains and no conscience."

"It's a queer story, but it's not illogical if you assume certain premises," said Warner thoughtfully. "Arguing that Vivian Lestrange is the man she describes—a man with a morbid desire for secrecy—this Eleanor Clarke is just the sort of woman who would have suited him as a secretary. She had no family, and wasn't of a gregarious disposition. The circumstances of her life might well have bred in her a habit of secretiveness, and the two queer lonely creatures may have found one another very satisfactory. I'm prepared to accept all that unless we find any discrepancies in the story. There's another point that occurs to me. You'd better find out for certain that Eleanor Clarke's father really died."

Bond's jaw dropped, and he stared at the other with incredulous eyes.

"That's a bit far-fetched," he protested, and then fell into a muse. "Funny business, all of it," he commented. "She says the father's name was John Clarke, and that he was killed by a horse which threw him and rolled on him. That's over twenty years ago, and Australia's developed a bit since then. However, I'll have it looked into."

"You see, Vivian Lestrange knew Australia pretty well,—or he wrote as if he did," said Warner. "You never know. The story may fit together in a way we hadn't foreseen."

"It's also worth while remembering that Eleanor Clarke knew Australia, and could have written about it from first hand knowledge," said Bond.

Warner nodded. "I grant you that," he said. "Don't think I'm minimising your theory. You've formulated a reasonable judgment in a scientific way, and nothing you have found in your investigation up till now invalidates your original theory. Taking Eleanor Clarke as a woman with unusual literary ability, she could have done all that you have suggested. First, she wrote *The Charterhouse Case*: then, when it was published, and had achieved a striking success, she laid her plans for this double personality business. She taught herself to write with her left hand, and enlisted Mrs. Fife as her accomplice. Having opened the banking account with the publisher's reference to cover her tracks, she took the lease of Temple Grove and invented Mr. Thomas Browne. Meanwhile, she herself lived in a separate establishment near by, going to Temple Grove every day in the guise of the secretary. It's not impossible, but if it's true, the woman must be quite abnormal. The whole thing is so elaborate and has gone on for so long. If she has done what you suggest there must be some other motive behind it all."

"I've been reading those Lestrange books," said Bond. "I don't pretend that my literary judgment is worth tuppence,—I know it isn't,—but I can't help thinking that the complexity of those stories argues an ingenious and tortuous mind. If Eleanor Clarke invented the Lestrange mysteries, this little game would be child's play to her. Those novels are simply amazing, and every detail in them is thought out to the limit of probability. There's not a slip of any kind, at least, not in the parts I'm capable of judging. Compare them with the average mystery story,—the difference is astonishing."

"You're perfectly right, Bond," replied Warner. "Now let's carry on along your lines, assuming that Eleanor Clarke is Vivian Lestrange and vice versa. We say the whole thing's a bluff and our investigation is simply a cause of mirth to the person who let us in for it, therefore we'll do nothing further. Is the situation going to stop there,—just fizzle and die like a damp squib?"

"No, confound it! It's not!" burst out Bond indignantly, "and don't I know it! I prophesy that Miss Clarke's next move will be to enlist the Press on her side. Imagine the head lines! 'Where is Vivian Lestrange? Police lethargy! Famous author victim of foul play.' My holy aunt!" he groaned. "She's got us at the end of a string, and we've got to dance on it for her amusement!"

Warner nodded. "Once again you're perfectly right. This story has got to be followed up and proved or disproved, if only to save our own faces. If anybody enlists the Press, we must. I admit that it will be just the advertisement the young woman

desires if your theory is right, but one point emerges. If she
sticks to her guns she can't profit financially. She can't touch the
Lestrange royalties, and she can't go on writing the Lestrange
books. She's cooked her own goose."

"She'll easily get over that," said Bond morosely. "When
she's got the whole Press fairly going, she'll have a nervous
breakdown, and then when she's recovered she'll announce that
the whole thing was a loss of memory and that she is Vivian
Lestrange after all, and if the police had had any sense at all
they'd have realised that she was ill to start with."

Warner laughed. "I've misjudged you, Bond. I thought you
were one of those practical, hard-headed fellows who didn't
indulge in flights of imagination. You not only observe facts, you
can imagine the development of them. Now you can set your
mind at rest about Miss Clarke's peculiarities in the leg-pulling
line. I'll see that she makes a sworn statement, and if she doesn't
stick to the truth, she can go into the dock on a charge of perjury.
Moreover, I'll have her interrogated by a nerve specialist and an
alienist. If she's bluffing she'll find her bluff is going to be called
with a vengeance. That's the procedure to meet the case if your
theory holds water, and the verdict is, 'he laughs best who laughs
last.' Now for the opposition theory."

"Right," said Bond, looking mollified at last. "I'm only too
anxious to look at the case all round, provided I'm satisfied that
that nimble-witted woman doesn't get away with it."

"She shan't,—and that's that," said Warner. "We are now
going to assume that Vivian Lestrange is a tall, bearded man
of about fifty, with a passion for concealing himself, not only
from his publishers, but from observation of any kind. Taking
his existence for granted, what do you make of the evidence?"

Bond sat up and squared his broad shoulders.

"First, no man of normal mind and health would conceal himself like that unless he were afraid of something," he began. "Either Vivian Lestrange has done somebody some vital injury and is afraid of getting his deserts, or else he is in fear of the law. His books are so sane that one can't put him down for an escaped lunatic, but there's nothing against the theory that he's a criminal hiding from justice."

"Excellent," said Warner. "You have covered the ground admirably. I'm reminded of that case at Southend last month when a defaulting solicitor was discovered in the guise of an author leading the simple life. He'd had quite a successful career as an author, too, before he was identified. Let us assume, for argument's sake, that Lestrange had committed some fraud, or some other criminal act before he took to writing. He may have given his secret away in his books and been traced through his publishers. However careful they were to respect his desire for secrecy, Langston's must have let some of their clerks know Lestrange's address, and it may have been given away by one of them. Also there is the missing housekeeper,—we mustn't forget her. What follows those assumptions?"

"That Lestrange was traced to Temple Grove, shot through the window, and removed, either dead or alive," replied Bond promptly.

"Exactly," said Warner, "though one must add that he may have bolted, after realising that his secret was no longer a secret. The salient points in this aspect of the case are the hole in the window, and the condition of the study. The latter suggests a careful cleansing to conceal any signs of the crime."

It was Bond who laughed a little this time. "I'm far from being a blood-thirsty man," he said. "I hate murders and I hate murderers, but I must admit that the discovery of a bearded corpse would give a fillip to my jaded mind."

Warner grinned. He had come to the conclusion that he liked Bond. The man was logical and thorough, and by no means so lacking in imagination as he appeared on the surface.

"The fillip in question is a bit remote at present," he said, "but we'll bear it in mind. Now judging from your report, Temple Grove doesn't look the sort of place that's susceptible to burglary. You got over the walls with ladders, but ladders are a bit too cumbersome to find favour with a man whose life is probably going to depend on his ability to avoid notice. I think it's probable that Lestrange's enemy got inside the wall by means of the door in it, and that involves the co-operation of Mrs. Fife—always assuming that Miss Clarke's telling the truth when she stated that she had no key to the premises. If the interloper had the key to the door in the wall, it's probable that he had the key to the house door as well. Now we come to the hypothetical shooting. It could have happened in various ways. The interloper could have come to the door of the study and potted at Lestrange as he sat at his desk. Similarly the shot could have been aimed through the study window. The alternative theory is that Lestrange saw his visitor and shot him at sight. There's no means of telling whether the window was broken from inside or outside I take it?"

Bond shook his head. "None at all. There were no fragments of glass either on the floor in the room, or on the path outside. Both surfaces had been swept and garnished as you put it."

Warner meditated for a little while.

"The next stage in our reconstruction involves the assumption of a corpse to be cleared away," he went on at last. "It seems improbable to me that one of the duellists—to use that expression—was wounded and just walked off. If Lestrange had been hurt there would have been no one in the house to help him bar the housekeeper..."

"And for all we know to the contrary, she may have shot him," said Bond succinctly.

"Lord! what a tangle," groaned Warner. "In either case, Mrs. Fife must have been accessory. I'm going to stick to the most obvious suggestions for the moment, Bond, or we shall drown in a quagmire of suppositions. Either Lestrange was shot, and the housekeeper helped to dispose of him, or else the interloper was shot by Lestrange..."

"—and the housekeeper obliged there too?" put in Bond mildly.

"Very well," said Warner. "Leave it at that. The next theory is that there was one corpse—unknown—and one housekeeper to assist in the doings. The next point was a large spring cleaning, in which I should say a woman had the initiative, seeing it was so thoroughly done. After that we assume a car outside the house, a guarded scouting of the roadway without, and a hasty shoving of inanimate passenger into the back of said car... either a roomy saloon, or better still, a nice big touring car, complete with waterproof cover over the rear seats, nicely buttoned down. No one ever asks what you've got under the cover...

"You know if this sedition bill goes through we shall be in clover... The covered-in rear seats of the plutocratic Packard arouse my sleuthing instincts. I shall be able to search for seditious literature or smuggled corpses at any hour of the day or night, provided someone muzzles the Socialist watchdog. Sorry. That was a digression."

"Quite," said Bond coldly. "To the best of our knowledge, Vivian Lestrange hadn't a car. He'd have found it too risky to buy one all in a hurry."

"That £400?" queried Warner pleasantly. "Cash down and no questions asked? A 1920 Rolls Royce or elderly Daimler? That's a nice little bit of routine which can be dealt with by my department."

"It seems to me that we're doing some pretty wild guessing," said Bond, "but having assumed a corpse, and knowing that there is no corpse on the premises, I favour the theory that the outsider did the shooting, having the car all ready beforehand. If Lestrange had shot someone on his own premises with the co-operation of Mrs. Fife, he could have buried the corpse in the garden and retired at leisure, first informing his secretary that he was going abroad for his health."

"Yes," said Warner thoughtfully. "It's like a game of permutations and commutations,—the possibilities are so numerous that one could spend a lifetime describing them. What a story Lestrange could have made of this... In the meantime have your men got hold of any information at all about cars outside Temple Grove, or any signs of movement there during the week-end?"

Bond shook his head.

"Nothing at all. Miss Clarke says that she left the house at five-thirty on Saturday afternoon and reached her flat ten minutes later. She did not go out again until Sunday afternoon, when she says that she went for a walk over to Ken Wood. She was seen re-entering her flat at Clare Court about four-thirty, but that's all the corroboration I can get about her statements. Mrs. Fife was at Temple Grove on Saturday afternoon as usual and, as I told you, left at her usual time. There's not a single detail to denote any abnormality during the week-end. Neither neighbours nor point-duty men can tell us a thing."

"Well, we've explored the unknown by the light of our imaginations," said Warner cheerfully. "Now we have got to concentrate our attentions on the known,—Miss Clarke and Mrs. Fife. First, I will arrange for the psychologist wallahs to investigate the fertile brain of your informant. When they have reported on her, the Press must be ranged on our side. I congratulate you on the amount of work you've got through, Bond. You've handled the preliminaries admirably. It will be interesting to see if we're handling a case for a psycho-analyst, a case of perjury, or a murder case."

Bond got up from his chair with a sigh.

"Well, if it's a murder case we're working on, I should like a body to get busy on," he said. "An inquest is a nice tidy logical business. I hate these Will o' the Wisp games."

"Said Bond—In a job of detection
I prefer things laid out for inspection.
With this evidence nebulous
I feel that incredulous
Go, get me a corpse for dissection."

chanted Warner. "Would the *Morning Post* give me half a guinea for that, on the principle of the Personal column limerick? The corpseless crime,—cops for the credulous, our incorporeal criminals and all that."

Bond grunted. "And a Clarke for a Chief Inspector," he added. "I expect you'll like her. There's no accounting for taste."

"*De gustibus*... I'm sure I shall. Clarke of Clare Court of course! This alliterative method is so lucid,—pattern making as Ellery Queen would put it. Very good, Bond! I'll get going on the psychopaths to make assurance doubly sure!"

"Very good, sir," said Bond sedately, and left the room without a smile.

CHAPTER V

"You have presented us with a very knotty problem, Miss Clarke," said Chief Inspector Warner, smiling in a friendly way at the lady whom he had described as "the pseudo authoress." Warner believed in studying people in their own environment, and he had called on Eleanor Clarke—without warning her of his coming—on the Tuesday afternoon, just over a week after she had made her first statement to Inspector Bond. She had received him quite coolly, without any sign of agitation, and was now seated opposite to him in her small sitting-room, studying him with steady, observant grey eyes.

"Since problems are your speciality, you might begin by considering the fact that this situation was something of a problem for me," she said dryly. "I have my living to earn, and I was very well content with the job I had got. I saw myself faced with the loss of that job, with no testimonial or reference to help me to get another one, and with the choice of breaking my promise to my employer, or being suspected by the police if there had been an accident—or a crime—at Temple Grove. I found it a very knotty problem, and having acted on the decision which seemed most sensible, I now find myself under suspicion of being an impostor, a nerve case, or a lunatic.

"I don't know if it's any use assuring you that those suspicions are unfounded. Inspector Bond certainly does not believe a word I have told him, and I have no means of proving that I have told the truth."

"From my point of view, you couldn't have made a better beginning to our interview," said Warner cheerfully. "I see your point of view perfectly, and I think we can simplify certain aspects of the problem if you will co-operate with us. You don't look to me a bit like a nerve case, and still less like a lunatic, but I am a layman, and my opinion isn't really authoritative."

Eleanor Clarke laughed outright. "You're rather refreshing," she said. "I like people who say what they mean, and I take it that you want an expert opinion on my own mental state? I'm quite willing to co-operate with you there, providing you are not planning to put me into a mental home unjustifiably."

"I should hate to do that," replied Warner, "and I also believe it's even harder to get someone sane put into an asylum, than it is to get someone insane out of one. I want to get you comfortably ensconced in the position of a witness whose bona fides is unquestionable. First, I suggest that you should consult a psychologist and nerve specialist,—who will give you, I am convinced, a certificate of fitness from his point of view; a very brief interview with an alienist will,—once again I speak with certainty—convince that practitioner that you are of no interest to him."

"How wisely you put it!" she said, laughter once again lighting up her face. "I'm quite willing to agree to that, for I'm not in the least afraid of being mistaken for a mental case by anybody who is not a bit of a mental case themselves. Of course your department will pay the specialist's fees.

"Finally, we come to the suggestion that I am an impostor. Is it true that you have a gadget like a blood pressure indicator, which rings an electric bell when the subject of examination tells lies? A veritometer, to coin a word?"

"No, I'm afraid we haven't,—not yet," said Warner; "any excursion in that direction might bring us up against the philosophers, and the immortal query of jesting Pilate... Our procedure in this matter is far from fool proof, but it's the best we can do at the moment. You make a sworn statement of your evidence before a commissioner for oaths, and we investigate your statement at leisure. In the event of discrepancies, we put you in the dock for perjury."

"I see," replied Eleanor Clarke. "As you say it's a *pis aller*, but I'm quite willing to oblige. I can't hold out to you the prospects of a conviction..."

"Don't distress yourself about that," said Warner earnestly. He was quite enjoying the conversation, and the cool flippancy of his *vis-à-vis* amused him, whereas it merely irritated Bond. "It's always very difficult to study other people objectively," went on Warner, "one is biased by one's personal convictions, however impartial one tries to be. Now you have set us the task of trying to find Vivian Lestrange... That's what it amounts to, isn't it?"

"You can put it like that if you wish," she replied. "When I walked into the police station, I had two motives in doing so. I wanted to do something to help Mr. Lestrange—assuming that he had been attacked—and I wanted to put myself straight with the police in the event of future trouble."

"Yes. I see that clearly enough," replied Warner, "and you were perturbed at the outset by Bond's quite comprehensible theory that he had found Vivian Lestrange in yourself. So far as I am concerned, my personal bias makes me view the case in a different light. I can't believe that any woman wrote *The Charterhouse Case*, or any of the other Lestrange books. Hence I'm not expecting you to be convicted of perjury along those lines. If I am proved to be wrong, my *amour propre* will suffer a nasty jar."

Once again Eleanor Clarke laughed wholeheartedly.

"The inevitable bone of contention again!" she retorted. "I won't waste your time by arguing about it, but I am beginning to regret that I inherited an honest disposition from honest parents. Think of the fun I could have had if I had assumed the mantle of Vivian Lestrange publicly. It would have been quite easy,—and all your literary amateurs would have been so annoyed, having your ready-man-made theories burst up for you!"

"Exactly!" agreed Warner promptly. "So far as I can see, your present position seems most unprofitable,—and that's why I'm here to try to collect evidence about a man whom I believe to exist and who,—it is alleged—has disappeared completely."

"That blessed word 'allegation,'" murmured Eleanor Clarke, with a lift of her fine level brows. "However, since you are willing to take my allegations seriously, I can assure you wholehearted co-operation in the leisurely investigation you propose."

Warner's eyes twinkled as he replied,

"And now, having cleared the ground, let's get down to it! You have been secretary to Vivian Lestrange for three years, and I'd hazard a guess that you are an observant person. I want you to tell me all that you know, or have surmised, about your employer during that time. Be as detailed as you like. I'm a good listener."

Eleanor Clarke lighted a cigarette thoughtfully before she replied, pushing the cigarette box across to Warner and waiting for him to light up before she began speaking.

"Mr. Lestrange is a man of about fifty," she said. "He is about five feet ten in height, but he stoops considerably. He must have been well built and powerful originally, but now he limps a bit and is awkward in his movements. I should say that his limp and stiffness are due to rheumatism or the early stages of arthritis, rather than to any injury, because on some days he moved much more freely. On his bad days he generally wore a thick dressing-gown and liked to have the room much too warm for my liking. He has a pleasant voice, low and deep, with a slight hesitation—not exactly a stammer—when he begins a sentence. From his voice I should have put him down as a university man—Oxford for preference. I once tried to ascertain that point by talking enthusiastically about Cambridge. All that I discovered was, that he knew both places well."

Warner chuckled a little, and she went on,

"As I told Inspector Bond, when I went to Temple Grove first, I thought Mr. Lestrange was a crank. He laid so much emphasis on his anonymity, and I found something pathetic in it. He was also very meticulous over the arrangements of things in his study, and insisted on everything being put in exactly the same place always."

Warner here made a note in the notebook he had produced and she said,

"I think I can guess the query you intend to make,—were things in their usual place on Monday evening? Yes, they were. Nothing was disarranged at all... Of course, as I got to know Mr. Lestrange, I changed my first estimate of him. I realised that his books were so well known that if his identity and address became public property, he would be plagued with a lot of visitors and invitations which he would simply loathe. I think he is a very sensitive man and also a very shy one, and he valued the uninterrupted peace which his habit of life ensured."

"Yes," said Warner, leaning forward in his chair. "I see that you would have grown accustomed to a strange situation, and have taken it for granted eventually, but when you first went to Temple Grove, didn't you indulge in any wild surmises to account for the situation? You told Bond that Lestrange never went out, never received visitors, and never wrote any private letters. It must have struck you as odd."

"It certainly did," she replied, "and if you are interested in my wild surmises, I'll tell you about them. All my guesses were pretty obvious ones, including the theory of an escaped convict,—but if he had been that, he would never have written a description of Dartmoor to draw attention to himself. He obviously was not a mental case, for his mind was singularly clear, but his assumption of invalidism intrigued me a bit. Most invalidish men like a doctor to fuss over them, but Mr. Lestrange never had a doctor in the house. He had a feverish cold last winter and was obviously pretty ill, but he refused point blank to see a doctor."

"What did the housekeeper have to say about that?"

"Mrs. Fife? She was always very taciturn to me, and when I told her she was taking a risk in not getting in a doctor she told me to mind my own business pretty sharply. She added that she knew a good deal about nursing and didn't want any advice from me. She certainly seemed devoted to Mr. Lestrange, and took endless trouble for him... Tell me, have you found out where she lives?"

Warner shook his head. "No, we can't discover a single thing about her. Like her master, she has simply vanished."

"Really, the whole thing's a nightmare," she said. "I shall honestly be glad to see your psycho-analyst, because I'm beginning to doubt my own sanity."

"Oh no! you mustn't disappoint me like that," said Warner plaintively, "besides we have independent evidence that Mrs. Fife really functioned. The greengrocer's boy has seen her open the door at Temple Grove to let you in, so we can't suppose that Mrs. Fife was merely another aspect of your own interesting personality."

"Thank you for those few kind words," she replied, her lips twitching with amusement. "I'm sorry that I'm being so dull. I feel that I ought to have something spectacular to tell you, but life at Temple Grove was the quietest sort of existence. Nothing exciting ever happened except in the books of Vivian Lestrange."

"Tell me exactly what did happen," said Warner. "Give me a typical day's work."

"I arrived at ten every morning," she replied, "and was admitted by Mrs. Fife. I went upstairs, took off my outdoor things and left them in the room arranged as my dressing-room on the first floor; then I went to the study, and invariably found Mr. Lestrange sitting at his desk. Sometimes he gave me a pile of manuscript which he had written since I had left on the previous day; sometimes he got me to read aloud some chapters which I had already typed, and we used to discuss various points. He liked to argue out his theories on characterisation, and often discussed the form of a sentence, getting me to look up points in Fowler and other books of reference. That is a detail which might interest you," she said suddenly. "You have read his books and you know that his literary style is not only beautiful, but his English is invariably correct. The one came from a natural gift, the other from taking a great deal of trouble. He had a natural sense of the use of words, but I often found him strangely ignorant of the rules which dictate that use. He would ask my opinion on all sorts of points—and then get me to verify it by a context."

"That's quite good," said Warner appreciatively. "He was neither a scholar nor a pedant by training."

Lighting another cigarette, she went on,

"Then he usually gave me a batch of letters to answer. A lot of people wrote to him—at Langston's address of course—and the letters fell into various categories. There were notes of appreciation or criticism, invitations and requests for interviews, begging letters and advertisements. The two latter he ignored, the others were always answered by the same sort of formula, expressed in the third person. 'Mr. Vivian Lestrange thanks Mr. So & So for his letter. The appreciation expressed therein has been a source of pleasure to the author.' I have never known him to spread himself in a letter, though some of those he received were genuinely interesting. However, to get on with my day's work. I did my typing in the study, and the sound of it never seemed to worry him, but I was never left alone in there. At one o'clock I generally went home for lunch and I returned to work at two. At four o'clock Mrs. Fife brought in tea, always a tray for him and a tray for me, and we discussed the work we were busy on at the time. Occasionally I tried to get him to talk about other things—the news in the paper, politics, religion or books. I found the result was always the same,—he would egg me on to express my own opinions, ask a lot of questions—often very shrewd ones and dismiss the subject without having committed himself to any opinion at all. I generally stayed until about half-past five and then went home."

Here she broke off for a moment or two, and leaned forward with her elbows on her knees, her chin in her hands. Warner leaning back in his chair, looking for all the world like a friendly visitor who had dropped in for a gossip, studied his companion without appearing to do so. He admired her slim, graceful figure and well-shaped hands and feet, and he liked the soigné effect of her well-fitting dark blue frock with the little lawn collar fitting the base of a really beautiful throat; the boyish style of hair-cut suited her admirably, and Warner thought how charming it looked in contrast to the over-elaborate "long-short" curls which disfigured so many modern heads; but it was not the attractiveness of her appearance that interested him, but the character which he was able to read behind it. The finely-shaped head, level brows and steady eyes were those of a thinker, and the firm lips and strong jaw told of determination and reserves of energy. She sat still, too, without any fidgeting, and her occasional movements were deliberate and well controlled. Turning from the woman herself to the room she sat in, he saw the same evidence of orderliness and grace. Plain grey walls, decorated with a few colour prints of the Post-Impressionist school, Gauguin and Van Gogh flower pieces; plain tables and chairs, the latter upholstered in grey corduroy, yellow silk cushion covers and curtains; a long, low bookcase filled with small uniform editions,—Hardy, Conrad and Jane Austen, Trollope and George Eliot, with the solid green of Galsworthy's later works,—all this fitted in with the picture of the self-contained thoughtful young woman who owned them. The room was perfectly tidy and innocent of knick-knacks or ornaments. A bunch of long-stemmed yellow Darwin tulips was the only extra decoration allowed and there was no sign of either gramophone or wireless.

After a moment's silence she turned to Warner again.

"When Mr. Lestrange first asked me to go to see Langston's and to pretend that I was he, I demurred. It seemed too much like sheer fraud, but he talked me round to his point of view. He said there was no reason why a writer's private life should be exploited for advertisement—as so often happens today; that neither public nor publisher needed to know anything more about a writer than was contained in his books, and that Mr. Marriott's demand for a personal interview to discuss a controversial passage was only camouflaged inquisitiveness. To which I replied, 'Then treat it as such and send him a polite refusal,' but Mr. Lestrange answered that he'd put Marriott and Bailley off so many times before, and they were becoming more and more insistent each time they suggested an interview. 'I *won't* go and see them,' he said, speaking with a sort of childlike obstinacy. 'I have worked in peace and quietness, for peace and quietness itself. I don't want to be bothered with them. Do this thing as a kindness to me, and I shall be infinitely indebted to you. Regard it as a joke—you're young and light-hearted, and you ought to be able to get a laugh out of it. You'll pull it off all right,—I'm not afraid there!'"

She shrugged her shoulders and looked at Warner defiantly. "As you know, I went," she said. "It was all very easy, because I had seen all Mr. Lestrange's correspondence with Langston's, I enjoyed it,—that I don't deny,—although I was ashamed, too, because Mr. Marriott was so charming to me, but afterwards, when I told Mr. Lestrange about it, he was so amused and delighted that I just didn't worry any longer. I knew he was a crank, but he was a very kindly, amusing crank."

"Yet even so, didn't you think that his behaviour was odd enough to require some explanation?" demanded Warner. "It's not fair to ask one's secretary to do impersonations of that kind."

"I know," she said slowly. "I did realise—at the back of my mind—that there must be some very strong motive for his secretiveness—that's partly what took me to the police station. I was afraid,—though I can't tell you what I'm afraid of."

Warner nodded. "That one occasion was the only time you did your famous impersonation, I suppose?" he asked.

"Oh, no! I went to dine at Mr. Marriott's flat and met Mr. Michael Ashe... It's worse and worse, isn't it? Mr. Marriott wrote the most charming letter addressed to Vivian Lestrange, Esq., as usual on the envelope, but containing an invitation to Miss Lestrange... After a lot more discussion the invitation was accepted and I spent a most exhilarating evening... I know it was underhand and an abuse of hospitality," she said sadly, "but I couldn't help enjoying it. Parties don't come my way as a rule, and this was a very piquant party! It was so evident that Michael Ashe didn't believe in me, but he couldn't say so outright, because he had to observe the convenances on account of Mr. Marriott and Mr. Bailley,—they're perfect dears, old-fashioned sticklers for etiquette, both of them. I registered a hope that I might never come across Ashe when I was alone; I have a feeling that I couldn't get away with it successfully under those conditions."

"Why?" said Warner bluntly. "If the two publishers had accepted you, why not Ashe?"

"Partly because he's conceited and believes no one's opinion if it's contrary to his own, and partly because there's an element of brutality in him. He has a veneer of courtesy, but once that wears thin, he is the type of man to make me see red with rage, and when one's angry, one is off one's guard."

Warner nodded.

"Yes. That's true enough. Did Mr. Lestrange express any interest in your party?"

"Oh, rather! He wanted to hear all about it, and was much amused with the conversation which I repeated verbatim as far as I could. He was hugely amused with the way I'd tackled Ashe, and seemed awfully pleased with me! In fact he raised my salary on the spot, although I told him I wouldn't oblige him again in the matter of understudying him."

"What did he say to that?"

"Oh, just laughed, and said that I had evidently done it so well that further demonstration should be unnecessary. I believe he was immensely amused to think that he'd thrown dust in people's eyes, and was rather pleased with his own astuteness."

Silence fell between the pair for a while, and then Warner said:

"You have been an exemplary witness so far, Miss Clarke. Personally I have found your narrative not only interesting, but convincing as well, and now I come to the most important question of all. Have you any suspicion that anything was out of the ordinary at Temple Grove during the last few weeks? When you did not get any answer to the bell on Monday morning, did you say in your mind, 'I expected something was going to happen. Now it's happened and I don't know what to do'?"

She shook her head. "No. I can answer that question quite definitely. I used to have that sort of feeling when I first got my job there. I've had a miserable time in offices which I've loathed, and I'd been out of work for nearly two months. Then, when I got this job which I enjoyed so much, I used to say to myself, 'It's much too good to be true. I expect the old boy's mad, or a bad hat, and it'll come to an end with a big bang.'… But it didn't. I'd been there for three perfectly good years, loving it all the time, and there was nothing in Mr. Lestrange's eccentricity that worried me at all. No. It was just when I felt most confident that everything was all right that this happened."

"And what did you think had happened?"

"I didn't know what to think. I had awful thoughts of the kind old boy lying dead, or hurt. I was simply distraught over it."

"Well," thought Warner to himself, "if this is acting, it's amazingly good acting…"

Aloud he said: "What rôle did Mrs. Fife play in your visions?"

"Certainly not a beneficent one," she replied. "I've nothing against her, she was very competent, and seemed devoted to her master, but I always felt she didn't trust me,—and didn't like me, either. Consequently I didn't like her. I always used to think I could see the satisfaction in her face when she saw me out of the house in the evenings. She always said 'Good evening, Miss,' most politely, but if she'd said what was in her mind, it would have been 'Good riddance.'"

"Another point that I wanted to ask you about was this," said Warner. "What holidays did you have?"

"My agreement gave me a fortnight a year and the usual Bank Holidays," she replied, "but for the last two years I've been given a month's holiday,—in June each year, because I wanted to go abroad. Mr. Lestrange paid me for the whole month and gave me a five pound note as well—you can imagine how sorry I am to have lost him!"

"You must be indeed," said Warner sympathetically, "and what did Mr. Lestrange do while you were away?"

"I never asked, and he never told me," she replied. "I always felt that one of the things which made me acceptable to him was that I didn't ask questions."

Warner smiled. "It's an unusual quality," he said. "Now Bond and I earn our living by asking questions and comparing the answers. In reply to some of his queries Bond has discovered that Temple Grove was shut up during the month that you were away. Whatever Mr. Lestrange and Mrs. Fife did during June of last year, they didn't stay at Temple Grove."

"Good gracious!" exclaimed Eleanor Clarke. "How did he find that out?"

"The butcher, the baker, the candlestick maker," chanted Warner. "In other words the milkman knows everybody's holidays. You can't leave twenty-eight bottles of milk to collect on the doorstep. You counter-order it to avoid such a contingency."

"How stupid of me!" she said. "You know I haven't the detective brain at all. I lack the touch of imagination which makes your brain ask How and Why? That's why I can't write novels—not for lack of words, but for lack of ideas. I believe I could produce pages of Vivian Lestrange's language by sheer mimicry, but I could never produce an idea. I can collate quite intelligently, but I can't originate."

"Now bearing in mind that Mr. Lestrange almost certainly went away for his holidays, doesn't it occur to you that he probably went out in the evenings and during the week-ends when you weren't there to see him?"

"I suppose so," she replied, "but I'm so bewildered over the whole thing that I don't know what to think next. Why can't you find Mrs. Fife? It's ridiculous to suppose that she's just vanished into thin air!"

"Quite ridiculous," agreed Warner, "and since we can find no trace of her at all, the only assumption is this. We haven't been able to get any information about a woman who had lodgings in Hampstead and who recently went away, because Mrs. Fife never did have lodgings in Hampstead. No one knows where she lived,—for the simple reason that she lived at Temple Grove."

"Good gracious!" said Eleanor Clarke, "but—" She broke off.

"Exactly," said Warner with his mischievous twinkle. "I expect she was quite glad to see you go home of an evening and to have the place to herself,—with her master for company."

"This," said Eleanor Clarke, "is a tale told by an idiot."

Warner laughed outright.

"Which is the idiot, you or me?"

"Neither," replied the other, "unless life makes idiots of us all."

"Oh, that I refuse to believe," said Warner. "My head is bloody but unbowed."

"If you have finished your exposition of the Inquisitorial and Oracular mind, may I offer you a cup of coffee? I am thirsty—and my brain is reeling."

"Thank you very much," said Warner. "A cup of coffee would be most acceptable."

CHAPTER VI

I T WAS TWO DAYS AFTER CHIEF INSPECTOR WARNER'S INTER-
view with Eleanor Clarke that Scotland Yard received information about the fire at Sir Duncan Grant's cottage; and Bond,
summoned to the Yard to discuss the matter with Warner, looked
less disgruntled than he had been doing recently.

"This gives us something to work on," he said cheerfully. "This
last week I've been chasing my own tail and getting nothing for it."

"You wanted a corpse to get busy on, and now you're supplied with one," said Warner, "though whether the specimen
they've provided at Ross will be really helpful, it's too early to
say. The bony portions of one solidly built Homo Sapiens leave
plenty to the imagination."

The facts were as follows. A farmer named Lewis, living at
Kirkham-on-Wye, Herefordshire, had informed the local policeman that there had been a fire at Sir Duncan Grant's cottage,—an
ancient stone built house in the Wye valley.

The cottage stood a couple of hundred yards back from the
river in a clearing in the woods which rose steeply up from the
fertile river-pastures. Lewis farmed the grasslands in the valley,
which were owned by Sir Duncan Grant, and he often cast a
friendly eye on the cottage—Kirkham Barns, it was called—on
behalf of the owner.

Grant, who lived in Ross, kept the cottage for use as a retreat
where he stayed for an occasional week-end to fish in the waters

of the Wye and to get a little rough shooting; but the place was unoccupied for the greater part of the year, and on account of its antiquity and lack of convenience it was somewhat despised by the inhabitants of the tiny village up above,—Kirkham was built on the crest of the hills on the right bank of the Wye.

Lewis, walking along the path by the river, intent on inspecting his pastures and considering the prospects of his stock, had just glanced up to the little clearing where stood the cottage, and what he saw made him gape. The cracked blackened windows and gaping roof told their own story—Kirkham Barns had been on fire and was now burnt out as thoroughly as its solid stone walls allowed. The farmer walked over the grass and pushed open the little gate in the wall which surrounded the small garden, and then stood by one of the windows and looked in. An acrid smell of burning filled his nostrils, and he could see that everything within the four walls of the cottage that could burn, had been reduced to charred fragments. The ceiling had fallen in and Lewis could see daylight through the gaping roof.

"Well, that's a pretty mess, that is," he soliloquised. "I wonder now... one of those tramps, as likely as not..." He stood with his ancient hat pushed back from his grizzled head and scratched his ear thoughtfully. It was a pity to see property destroyed, but he knew there was nothing of value in the cottage, and its ancientry made but small appeal to the unimaginative farmer. "A pretty mess, that be," was his verdict, as he turned away and continued his walk along the pastures. His inspection accomplished, he climbed the steep hill which led from the river valley to the village above, pondering over his discovery to the tune of an occasional "Drat that now!" Lewis had planned out his morning satisfactorily and he didn't want to put himself out. The nearest policeman lived at Ledwain, nearly three miles away,—but property was property and Sir Duncan Grant was his landlord. Lewis solved his problem by sending "the boy" into Ledwain on his bicycle with a short note which imparted the tidings to Walsh, the constable. Having done this, Lewis went about his morning's work without telling anybody else of his discovery. None of the villagers would bother to go down "the steep"—as the hill was called—unless they had some definite reason for going, and the rather dour farmer liked to keep his own counsel. In the afternoon of the same day Walsh arrived to inspect the cottage. Feeling that it was his duty to make a full report on the matter, he pushed aside the remains of the front door, and shook his head over the foul-smelling debris on the floor,—tiles and bedstead and crockery all tangled up together amid the charred beams and fallen plaster. The cottage was divided into two rooms on the ground floor and the dividing wall still stood—two solid feet of undressed masonry with the doorway at one end. Entering gingerly with a glance at the charred beams which still stretched above his head, Walsh went through the door space to the further room. This had been used as a kitchen and the twisted metal work of a small oil range stood on the flags. There was a large open chimney space in the stone wall and when Walsh set eyes on it, he gave a grunt of sheer consternation, and nearly turned tail and fled.

Forty years' service in the rural constabulary had not prepared him for a discovery such as this. Among the charred fragments in the open chimney there was something that had once been a human being; the fire had rendered the remains unrecognisable; whether a man or a woman had once inhabited that charred shell, Walsh could not tell—and he made no effort to find out. Going outside the cottage into the fresh sweetness of the April afternoon, he took off his helmet and mopped his brow. This sort of thing was strange to him, and he very definitely did not like it. Standing facing the river, he pondered over his next move; somebody more important than himself would have to enquire into this story,—but meanwhile there was no one at hand to act as messenger. The grasslands stretched unbroken for miles on either side and the nearest place to get assistance was the village of Kirkham "up the steep." Walsh, after another unhappy glance inside the cottage, (he rather hoped that he had been the victim of a delusion) trudged up the steep hill and made his way to Lewis's farm. After some argument, Walsh prevailed on the unwilling farmer to send a message to the Inspector at Ross, and the constable then walked down the steep once more, and stood guard over the ruined cottage until Inspector Foster came to join him. By the time the latter had arrived, Walsh had recovered from the shock of his discovery, and had begun to think things out. It was quite true,—as Lewis had suggested, that a tramp might have dossed down in the cottage—though tramps in the river valley were few and far between—but no tramp would have chosen to sleep in the open chimney space, presumably on top of the very fire which he had kindled for his comfort.

"Someone must ha' put that there," said Walsh to himself. "That" seeming a more suitable way of describing the human relic than the more problematical "him" or "her."

The upshot of the discovery was that a message was sent to Scotland Yard, telling of the gruesome discovery of unrecognisable male remains in Kirkham Barns. Chief Inspector Warner had recently sent out an "all stations" message, describing the missing author as fully as Eleanor Clarke's account allowed.

Superintendents had been requested to report immediately to the Yard in the event of any discovery which might seem to bear on the problem of the missing man.

Thus it came about that Warner and Bond discussed the news from Ross and its possible bearing on their researches.

"I shall go straight down there and look into it," said Warner. "The whole thing is a queer story, but if Lestrange were killed and his murderer is at large, I think I had better put a man on to keep his eye on Miss Clarke. She is the only person who can give us any information, and consequently she is a real menace to the murderer, if such there be."

"Yes, that's true enough," said Bond, "but there's another puzzle to face, sir. If Lestrange were killed, it looks as though the housekeeper must be a party to the crime. Why didn't Mrs. Fife send a message to Miss Clarke, telling her not to come to Temple Grove again until she received further instructions? That's a point which has bothered me all along."

"We've both been worrying away at this end of the story, like a dog with a bone," said Warner. "I'm hoping that this Ross find may give us a different angle for our observations. I could hazard a dozen different explanations of the Temple Grove story, only we have nothing to correct them by. Assumptions don't get us anywhere without concrete evidence."

"Well, the evidence up there sounds concrete enough," said Bond. "Let's hope that it fits in with some of your assumptions, sir."

When Warner arrived at Ross, he found two interesting pieces of news awaiting him. On examination of the calcined body found in Kirkham Barns, the Divisional Surgeon reported that a bullet had been found embedded in the brain. The second discovery was even more interesting. The remains of a sturdy, leather-bound pocket-book which must have been in one of the dead man's pockets had not been completely destroyed by the flames. Its leather cover had charred through, and most of the pages reduced to ash, but a few sheets in the middle of the closely-bound little volume still showed traces of handwriting. These had been treated by an expert and photographed, and Warner was able to recognise the queer, crabbed handwriting of Vivian Lestrange.

"Death caused… Carbon Monoxide… Hydrocyanic…" ran some of the decipherable words, and then "Varens killed on…" Detective-Inspector Foster was much intrigued by these suggestive fragments, but Warner only shrugged his shoulders.

"If that is Lestrange's body, one has got to remember that he was a writer and that his favourite theme is the mystery story. These jottings probably referred to some plot for a novel or short story. However, one thing is certain, the writing in that book is Lestrange's, and that fact connects up the body you have found here with the hypothetical writer we are seeking in London."

"Why hypothetical?" demanded Foster, and Warner replied:

"The only person who testifies to the existence of Vivian Lestrange is his secretary, Eleanor Clarke. Apart from her, no one has seen the man. Bond, who has been working with me, is still suspicious of Eleanor Clarke's good faith. His theory is that the so-called secretary is really the novelist and that her whole story is a cleverly contrived blind."

"Well, I'm jiggered!" exclaimed Foster. "That's a tall story, that is. How does he account for the body at Kirkham?—unless the novelist lady bumped off one of her friends, and then invented a character to fit the part."

Warner grinned. "That's the idea," he said, "but for the time
being I'm going to take the lady's word for it, and assume that
she is telling the truth, until I find evidence that she isn't. Now
before we set out, tell me a bit about this cottage, and any ideas
you've got on the subject yourself."

"Kirkham is seven miles from Ross by road," began Foster,
"and nine miles by the river. You can reach the cottage by two
ways,—either by going through the village of Kirkham and
descending the hill they call the steep, or else by following the
path by the river. If your witness is telling the truth, one can
assume that Lestrange was killed in London and his body trans-
ported here by car. Now I can't believe it's possible that anyone
took a car through Kirkham village and down the steep without
being noticed. It's a precipitous hill and only fit for farm carts to
go up and down. Although it's hard to say nowadays that any hill
is too stiff for a modern car to tackle, yet I don't believe that any
motorist would have taken the risk of a spill with a cargo like
that on board. No one has ever been known to get a car down
that hill yet, and I don't believe it's possible. Now take the other
alternatives. There's a road along the river valley from Ross to
Tenbury,—only that's three miles from Kirkham. After that
there's only a footpath, but it would be possible to take a car
all the way if you were careful, because the gates are all wide
enough to let the hay carts go through. The third possibility is
to go by car as far as Winyon, on the opposite bank of the river,
and then to borrow old Dick Barton's boat and reach Kirkham
Barns by water."

"Do you think that's possible considering all the circumstances?" asked Warner, and the other nodded.

"Yes. I'd say it was the least difficult on the whole. There's a lane which runs from the main road at Winyon straight down to the river by Barton's cottage. The old man's as deaf as a post, and he'd never hear a car at night. I know he leaves his oars in the boat out of pure laziness,—I've told him he deserves to lose the whole outfit. It might take the best part of half an hour to pull up the river with the stream against you, but you'd be pretty safe in Barton's old tub."

"In either case, we have one point to guide us," said Warner. "Anyone who succeeded in getting a corpse into Kirkham Barns must have been very well acquainted with the neighbourhood. In other words, there has been local talent on the job."

"You're right to some extent," said Foster. "That cottage is very far from being in the public eye. Kirkham is a tiny village—only a dozen houses in all, with no pub and no amenities for the tripper. Charries don't go there because the road is so narrow, and joy riders don't go there because you can't get a car down to the river. There are mighty few people who can be aware of the existence of that cottage by the river—only anglers, the village folk themselves, and Sir Duncan Grant and his friends."

"And that brings us to a point I've been thinking about on my journey up here," said Warner. "A few details about Sir Duncan Grant are indicated. I've looked him up in *Who's Who*. Age sixty, born in Monmouth, made a fortune out of munitions during the war, knighted for his services to the country, retired after turning his iron works into a company and is now among the ranks of the gentry. Said to have been 'privately educated,'—meaning self-made, I take it?"

"That's about it," said Foster with a grin. "However he's abroad at present."

"So much the better for him," returned Warner. "How long has he owned that cottage?"

"He bought some land after he was knighted, including Kirkham Barns, where his grandfather lived and brought up a family of six. In some ways Grant is rather a likeable chap; he's not in the least ashamed of his humble origin, for one thing, and he likes staying in that cottage all by himself and cooking his own food, and calling the villagers by their front names. It's people who come up against him in business who see the other side of the picture. He's as hard as nails and puts the screw on like a real Shylock."

"Well, I seem to have made a bowing acquaintance with the main facts," said Warner. "Now if you'll take me to the scene of action I should like to envisage the likeliest means of transporting corpses to outlying districts."

Getting into the police car with Foster, Warner set out for Kirkham. They took the main road to Monmouth and after about six miles, turned off along a narrow, untarred road, running between high hedges. As they climbed up steadily from the river they gained a magnificent view of the valley some three hundred feet below them, with the silver Wye twisting and turning between the woods, here spreading out into a wide sheet of water, there narrowing to a silver channel which ran swiftly between the steep banks. On both sides of the valley the ground rose to lofty hills which formed the skyline, and away to the south the grand contour of the Yat Rock reared its craggy heights against the sky. Warner sniffed the keen air appreciatively.

"I like this," he said. "There must be grand fishing in the river below there."

"Ay, the fishing's good enough," replied Foster. "There's salmon and trout in plenty. Sir Duncan lets some of his tenants fish in his waters, and you'll find the postman and blacksmith catching fine trout when the river's in flood. It's low now, more's the pity. We've had no rain for weeks."

"Are you an angler then?" asked Warner, and the other replied,

"Yes, but I wasn't thinking of that. If the river had been in flood lately, we should have had some tracks in the soft ground by the river side to tell us if a car had been along the dales. The hay's only just starting to grow and the ground is dry and hard. Still, there should have been tracks if a car had been driven from Tenbury to Kirkham Barns,—and there aren't any. That's why I favour old Barton's boat."

The village of Kirkham turned out to be even smaller than Warner had anticipated. He saw the two farm houses, six cottages and two other fair sized houses, comely old buildings with their half-timbered walls and mullioned windows. A tiny church and still tinier school completed the count, and Warner asked how many children went to the school. "About a dozen,— sometimes less," said Foster. "The school mistress has a soft job I reckon,—she lives in that cottage yonder—a nice little place."

Leaving the car outside Lewis's farm, the two men turned down the steep, and Warner understood why Foster had said that it was impossible to drive a car down the hill. The ground fell at a slope which Warner assessed at one in four, and the surface of the lane was rutted in miniature river beds, showing how the rain raced down in a torrent after a storm. In places the soil and loose stones were all washed away and the living rock gleamed under the trickle of water which flowed across to drain into the ditch on the eastern side, for the drain was biased laterally as it descended the hillside. The banks were gay with primroses, anemones and violets, and white blackthorn shone among the young foliage of hazel and larch, the latter marvellously green in the tender afternoon light.

"I say this is a damn fine spot," said Warner. "It's almost too good to be true, considering the way the countryside's being urbanised. Old Grant will be pretty sick about his cottage being mucked up. If once you got to care for a spot like this, I can imagine you'd just worship it."

"He's got plenty of money to put it to rights," replied the other prosaically. "He'll need it, too. They'll have to bring every-thing across the river. The farmers won't let any lorries through the meadows to spoil the hay. There you are. That's it."

Kirkham Barns looked very desolate with its gaping and blackened roof silhouetted against the glorious green of a larch wood. Thrushes were piping in the coppice, rabbits scuttled gaily in the little clearing between the cottage and the trees and the stream tumbling down the hillside added the music of running water. Damson trees in full flower shone like snow in the little garden, and Warner gave vent to his feelings in an exclamation of "What a damned shame! I hate fires,—they make such a sordid mess." Then he recovered his professional instincts and said: "Have you any idea when the fire occurred?"

"I've been trying to fix it," replied Foster, "but it's difficult. At this time of year there's no work in the pastures to bring the farmers down here. In a week or two they'll be bringing the young heifers down to grass, but at present the whole place is just left to itself. The children are in school until four o'clock, and then they have jobs to do for their parents. No one in the village came past here last Sunday, and we haven't had any reports in to help us. The place was all right a week ago last Sunday and that's all I can tell you. It must have been fired during the night and burnt itself out by morning. The wind's been from the north all the week and that would have blown the smoke away from the village. I've been making enquiries on the other side of the river, thinking the place must still have been smoking in daylight, but I've not had any luck so far."

Warner looked across the river valley towards the woods on the further side. The only house he could see was a long low building half way up the rise and Foster saw his eyes rest on it.

"That's Farwardine Manor," he said. "No one lives there. It's been empty for years."

"Somebody knew what they were doing when they came and dumped a corpse in that cottage," said Warner. "About as good a spot as they could find in England for a job like this."

"Maybe, but there's a lot about it that puzzles me," said Foster. "Whoever did it must have known that discovery couldn't be delayed for very long,—the body was certain to be found. If I'd managed to bring a corpse all this way, I'd have gone a bit further and chucked it into one of the deep holes in the caves beyond Symonds Yat. It might have stayed there till Judgment Day."

Warner was silent and thoughtful as he entered the cottage and surveyed the open chimney space from which the body had been removed.

"It's a matter of using one's imagination to account for the facts," he said. "One of the problems that occurs to me is this. Why didn't the murderer arrange his properties in such a way that one might have assumed that the whole thing was an accident? If the body had been laid on the floor—or on a table,—one might have assumed that a tramp had taken shelter here, lighted the oil stove for warmth and tumbled over it while he was half asleep. The fact that the body was found in the fireplace rules out any idea of accident at once... How would this fit the case? The culprits never intended the whole cottage to burn. They wanted to render their victim unrecognisable, and they decided to cremate him for that purpose, but they arranged their funeral pyre in the chimney space, intending it to turn out like an ordinary fire, and leave no traces which would be noticed from outside the house. You say that Grant is abroad. If the cottage hadn't caught fire, no one would have investigated the inside until Grant came back here for a week-end,—and then he would have discovered the body... You know, I can't help feeling hopeful that Grant may be able to give us a little assistance. Nobody chose this cottage by chance, the whole thing must have been carefully calculated."

"That's a very sound idea of yours about the fireplace," said Foster. "That chimney space is large enough to roast an ox. If your idea's the right one, the murderer probably overdid the flare-up by pouring paraffin or petrol on to the logs before he set them alight, and then the blaze got out of control and the whole show caught fire."

"Another point," said Warner. "Do you think this affair could have been the work of one man?"

Foster pondered. "He'd have had to be a pretty powerful fellow if he did it single handed," he said. "Corpses aren't easy to move, and this one must have been a tidy weight,—at least twelve stone."

Warner nodded, and led the way out of the blackened little building, glancing at the thickness of the walls.

"How old do you reckon this place is?" he asked in passing.

"Three hundred years, more or less,—probably more," replied Foster and then added, "I wonder if I could lift you out of a boat and ram you in that fireplace."

"Depends if you've mastered the trick of a fireman's lift," said Warner, "but, as you say, it wouldn't have been easy. In this case we've got to assume that Lestrange was shot in his study at Temple Grove and his body lifted into a waiting car. That argues the presence of two people to my way of thinking,—one to keep a look-out and one to do the lifting. I may be wrong there, for Temple Place is about the quietest little cul-de-sac in London. After that, the car—plus Lestrange's body—was driven to Ross—probably on the Sunday night. Wait a minute though… If the murderer drove west on Sunday night, he'd have had to loiter around most of Monday, because he wouldn't have risked starting his bonfire in the daylight."

Both men stood looking at the river, deep in thought, and then Warner said,

"When Vivian Lestrange concealed his identity with such care, I wonder if he realised that he was offering hostages, not to fortune, but to murder. In any murder case, the identity of the victim is the starting point. Here we've got a name and nothing else; we've got to make contact with someone who knew the man behind the name, and then we shall be able to fit our evidence to the personalia. At least we can start from this,—somebody who knew Vivian Lestrange also knew this cottage, and they left a body in it as a present for Sir Duncan Grant… Let's go and have a look at old man Barton and his boat, to give my imagination a little more to feed on, and then I want to find some local pundit who will remember all the scandals of a lifetime."

"You're arguing that Vivian Lestrange was a native of these parts?"

"Not of necessity, although there's evidence in his books that he knew this district pretty well. Read them yourself, and then you'll know as much as I do. Vivian Lestrange seems to have materialised from nowhere about three years ago, and his career ended abruptly in Kirkham Barns. We have to use our imaginations to account for the few facts we can depend on. Otherwise we shall get no further."

"Well, I'm glad you're lending a hand," replied Foster. "Guessing's not my long suit."

And with that the two men turned their backs on the river, and toiled up the steep ascent back to the village.

CHAPTER VII

AFTER DINNER THAT EVENING WARNER WENT TO CALL ON Mr. Vargon, an old solicitor who lived in a fine house in the open country just north of Ross. Scotland Yard can generally provide introductions to the man of law in any part of England, and Warner was greeted in a friendly manner by the fine old man with whom he had been recommended to make acquaintance. Hilary Vargon was an impressive figure, very tall and thin, with broad shoulders—much stooped, a long lean face, plentiful white hair and a massive head. He was dressed in loose baggy tweeds, and Warner felt that he would have looked equally at home in academic dress in a don's common room, or clad in waders, casting a fly on the river. The old man's voice was remarkably deep,—a musical rumble that was pleasant to the ear, and his blue eyes were very bright as he surveyed the Chief Inspector when they had settled down in big chairs on either side of a roaring log fire.

"I take it you're claiming our local corpse," he said. "You're welcome to it. Murder's more popular in London than it is here."

"I wouldn't say that," said Warner, "only our criminals are a bit more subtle than your west country lads. They've a habit of complicating the matter by covering up identities. I'm perfectly willing to believe that the chap your men found in Kirkham Barns is the one we've been puzzling over in London, only the evidence is a bit slender at present. Now if you'd like to hear our part of the story, I should be glad to know if it suggests any connecting links with affairs which have come into your province up here."

"Carry on," said Vargon. "I've had a finger in a good many queer pies during thirty years' practice in this part of the world, as well as hearing of some funny stories which never come into the courts. Whether I can help you in this affair is a different matter, I assure you I'll do my best. Try a cigar if you like them, and the whisky's all ready when you want a refresher."

"You have heard of Vivian Lestrange?" began Warner, and the other nodded.

"Yes. Yes. A clever fellow."

"According to our present information, Vivian Lestrange's history began rather over three years ago, when he sent *The Charterhouse Case* to Langston's, the publishers. Some months later Lestrange opened a banking account, and then took a house called Temple Grove, in Hampstead. Shortly afterwards he engaged a woman-secretary named Eleanor Clarke, who came in daily, and the pair seem to have worked together very happily. Lestrange was quite unknown in his own neighbourhood, apparently he never went out, and he received no visitors. He was so anxious to remain concealed from observation that he persuaded his secretary to impersonate him to his publishers. The only other member of the household was Mrs. Fife,—a woman who, according to evidence, came in daily from eight a.m. till eight p.m. as housekeeper. On Monday of last week, the secretary, Miss Clarke, went to the local police station and said that she was unable to obtain admission to her place of employment, and that the housekeeper was not known at the address she had given in Hampstead. Subsequent investigation by the police proved the house to be empty, and Lestrange and

Mrs. Fife missing. The whole house was unreasonably well polished and a french window leading on to the lawn was open, with a hole which might have been made by a bullet through the glass. In conclusion I must tell you that according to Miss Clarke, Lestrange always wore gloves, wrote with his left hand, and was absolutely unwilling to meet even his own publishers face to face. We have found no trace of either the housekeeper or of Lestrange up till the present time—unless the remains at Kirkham Barns are his—the pocket-book found on the body undoubtedly contains Lestrange's handwriting."

"That's quite a refreshing story," rumbled Vargon. "Nearly as original as Lestrange's novels."

Warner laughed. "Yes, sir,—but when a man has as fertile a mind as that man had, there's no need for him to stage tricks of this kind for advertisement. Given the facts as I have stated them, what construction do you put on them?"

"Obviously the man was hiding from somebody," said the lawyer. "A warrant may have been out for his arrest, or he may have escaped from gaol, or he may have been hiding from the vengeance of someone he had wronged."

"Let us take those points in order," said Warner, "there are warrants out which have never been executed but so far as we have ascertained at present, none of the wanted men seem to fit Lestrange's description. Neither has any man broken gaol and got clean away. The third point obviously remains an open question. I add another possibility,—that Lestrange is—or was—a man who had been in gaol, served his sentence, and started life again under a fresh name and identity."

"Yes, that's quite a reasonable deduction," agreed Vargon, "but the secrecy of his manner of living seems to indicate some sort of fear. If a man has served his sentence he has nothing more to fear from the law,—he's had his punishment, and can count himself all square. In this case it looks as though your man were hiding from some private vengeance."

"The fact—if Miss Clarke is to be believed—that Lestrange always wore gloves is a point which needs consideration," said Warner. "Either he was anxious to avoid leaving finger-prints, or else his hands had some peculiarity or mutilation, by which they could be recognised. Either explanation indicates that his fear of recognition was concerned with the police. Inspector Bond—the local man—puts another explanation forward; he argues that Vivian Lestrange and Eleanor Clarke are identical, and that the secretary is pulling our legs for reasons of her own."

"Meaning that she wrote *The Charterhouse Case*?" growled Vargon. "I don't believe it. That was a man's work."

"I quite agree with you," said Warner, "but it's worth while remembering that Langston's, the publishers, who have so much more opportunity than ourselves of assessing a problem such as this—are not of the opinion that it is possible to be dogmatic over it. Many a woman has written under a man's name and it has not been her literary work which has given the secret away. However, it's no use changing horses in mid-stream; I'm working on the principle that a man named Vivian Lestrange has disappeared and that his secretary is the only person known to us at present who could identify him. I come to you because I hope that you can think of some incident connected with anyone up here who might have had a motive to commit a murder. Bearing in mind that Vivian Lestrange was possibly once in prison—or feared that he might be arrested, can you remember any scandal or cause célèbre in this part of the world which might suggest murder as its possible culmination?"

Vargon stretched out his long limbs at full length in his roomy chair, clasped his hands behind his head and with elbows akimbo gazed up at the ceiling.

"That's a tall order," he said, "but give me a little while to cast around."

For some minutes they sat in silence, while Warner puffed away at his cigar, his mind busy visualising the house in far off Hampstead, and trying to imagine a connected narrative which would bridge the gap between the study in Temple Grove and the cottage in Kirkham. He was startled from his reverie by the older man suddenly sitting up with a jerk, banging a clenched fist on an open palm and exclaiming, "By jingo! That might do!"

"Good!" said Warner. "The oracle has answered! Let's have it!"

"It's pure guess work, but I've remembered one story that might fit the facts... In 1923 a warrant was issued for the arrest of two brothers, Edward and James Merstham. They were men of independent means, living in a fine old house near Tintern, and they were joint trustees in administering the estate of a boy named Carlyon. This boy was the son of a wealthy Cardiff merchant, Jesse Carlyon, a relative of the Mersthams; he died leaving his fortune in trust for his only son, then a boy of ten; the Merstham brothers were the trustees, whose business it was to administer the estate until the boy came of age.

"To cut a long story short, the boy was killed in a hunting accident and the Mersthams had to give an account of their trusteeship. You can read the case in detail for yourself but the salient facts were these. There was a discrepancy of £20,000 in the securities of the Carlyon estate,—somehow between them, James and Edward Merstham had embezzled the money. Edward was arrested, charged, and sentenced to seven years' penal servitude. James got clean away. Now one of the interesting points about this story is this; Edward not only pleaded 'not guilty,' but he swore he was the victim of his brother's double dealing. Edward admitted that certain monies in the Carlyon estate had been realised,—after considerable consultation between himself, James, and their brokers,—for the purpose of reinvestment. The sum realised was paid into Edward's banking account, earmarked 'Carlyon estate.' That was all straightforward. The trouble arose from the fact that the sum in question had been drawn out of the bank again by a cheque signed by both brothers, and paid into the account of some so-called broker in Mincing Lane, whence it had completely vanished, in company with the broker and James Merstham. That's the bald outline of the story. It seems to me that it's worth your while to look into it for at least three reasons.

"When Edward Merstham was sentenced he made a statement reiterating his own innocence, and swearing that James—who was the real culprit, should suffer for his sins one day. Another point is that the Mersthams were keen fishermen and they knew that stretch of the river by Kirkham Barns. Finally, Edward Merstham was released from prison after serving his sentence some four years ago."

"Yes," agreed Warner. "It looks as though we might make the cap fit. I was certain when I learnt that the pocket-book found in the Kirkham fire had Lestrange's writing in it that the problem had been narrowed down to an angle that made its ultimate solution probable. The number of people who know that cottage must be so limited that it narrows our enquiry into workable proposition automatically. Now let us see if we can fit the Merstham brothers to the facts."

"You'll be able to get all the details you need about Edward from the prison authorities," said Vargon, "but I can give you a rough idea of the pair of them. In 1923, Edward was forty years of age and James a few years younger. They had both been through the war, James having seen service in Mesopotamia and Salonica; Edward only home service, as his physique was not over good. After the war they lived together in the house they inherited from their parents, and lived the usual life of country gentlemen of independent means. It appears that their prosperity was only skin deep. When the Carlyon trust was examined for probate, it was assumed that the Merstham property would have made good the deficit. Not a bit of it. The two brothers were found to be practically insolvent, for most of their parents' money had been invested abroad, and most of it had vanished in Russia and Germany, and the remainder in ill-advised speculation in foreign currency. It was generally believed that the Mersthams had helped themselves out of the trust monies and that they had intended to decamp in any case. James was already abroad when young Carlyon was killed, and Edward tried to bolt too, but was arrested in Paris. According to his plea at the trial he was endeavouring to find James, in order to discover what had happened to the trust money."

"What was your own opinion of the matter?" asked Warner, and Vargon replied,

"I believed that James was the active rogue and Edward the passive. In other words, Edward knew that James intended to indulge in a little sharp practice for their mutual benefit, and Edward, being a vague sort of optimist, hoped it would be all right on the night. Of course it was the sudden death of young Carlyon that cooked their goose. The same thing has happened scores of times,—you can manipulate funds for years provided you pay the income due on them; it's the unexpected audit that shows you up. Edward pleaded that his signature on the later cheques was forged, and I daresay he was right, but that doesn't satisfy me that Edward was impeccable.

"James had the brains of the outfit; he was a very clever fellow. He used… by the Lord—here's another bit of evidence for you. James Merstham used to write a bit; he had more than one article in the *Western Mail*—descriptions of the countryside and fishing stories, and some old romantic adventures. You look up the files of the *Mail* for 1923. You'll find some of James' work to study."

Warner's eyes were bright with interest as he leaned forward alert to take in every word his companion uttered.

"I know it's no good jumping to conclusions," he said, "but the theory is such a good one that I can't help trying it out. One assumes that James Merstham, after having retired with the proceeds of his embezzlement, took to writing, the hobby with which he had amused himself when he lived in these parts. Presumably he kept out of this country for some years, until he was satisfied that the police would no longer be on the alert, and then he returned and settled down and took seriously to literature. His secret manner of life can be attributed to two causes,— his fear of the police and his fear of his brother Edward."

"And to complete the story, you assume that, in spite of all James' precautions, Edward eventually ran him to earth, shot him, and brought his body back to their native heath!" growled the lawyer. "If that's your case, I'm prepared to pick holes in it."

"Pick away," said Warner cheerfully. "That's where you can help me."

"First of all, I can't see James Merstham, who was one of the most energetic rogues that ever walked, fitting into the life of a sedentary recluse," objected Vargon. "James was a pretty lively fellow, a good hand with a gun and a line, and a rare runner after petticoats. I should like to have a few words with the secretary girl on that subject."

Warner laughed. "Objection noted. The secretary seems to me a likeable, straightforward young woman, and she appears to be telling the truth, but granting that, one must bear in mind that she only had the opportunity to see one side of the picture. It seems obvious that her employer stayed at home and worked during working hours. We have no proof that he never went out of an evening, or during week-ends. Temple Grove is situated in one of the quietest cul-de-sacs in London, the fact that his neighbours have never noticed Lestrange going in and out, is no proof that he didn't do so. Another point that arises is this. We haven't been able to find a trace of the housekeeper, Mrs. Fife. The local men have been remarkably efficient in the scope of their enquiries, but the fact remains that they can't get any information at all. My own private and personal conclusion is that Mrs. Fife lived at Temple Grove,—lived with Lestrange, that is to say."

Vargon's shrewd eyes twinkled.

"Quite a reasonable supposition, but where is she now, might I ask?" he replied. "I understood that there was only one corpse in the chimney,—not a brace."

"Only one," replied Warner. "The case of the missing house-keeper seems to land us in an 'either—or' predicament. Either she was killed to keep her quiet, or else she was in the plot. She found out Lestrange's secret and gave him away, and she's being paid to keep quiet."

"Who's paying her?" queried Vargon.

"Why, Edward Merstham. That is going on the assumption that Edward managed to cache part of the missing £20,000 before he was caught."

The lawyer lit another cigar thoughtfully before he replied.

"That's possible," he replied, "but Edward Merstham, for all his vagueness, would have the sense to know that his life would never be safe while a woman was sharing his secret. He'd have no hold over her."

"Yes, he would, if you put the case like this," replied Warner. "If Mrs. Fife is still alive, and knows that Lestrange was murdered, she has made herself an accessory. If she has taken money from the murderer she has already put herself outside the law. On the one hand she has a lump sum down, and a hope of more in the future; on the other she has only the prospect of being charged as accessory or principal. As things stand now, if she puts in an appearance she'll have an almighty difficult job to prove that she had no hand in the murder herself. If things were as I think they were, that household wasn't what you'd call a regular one."

"Well, the situation you're assuming is that James Merstham was settled in Temple Grove, hiding away from the world in general and from his brother in particular, but that somehow Edward tracked him down. Now, how in the world do you imagine that Edward succeeded in finding him?"

Warner laughed. "Considering it's only a few minutes ago that I first heard of the Merstham brothers, and considering the possibility that Lestrange was a reincarnation of brother James, you can't reasonably expect me to have ready made theories to explain away the difficulties. I can only tell you of the ideas that occurred to me before the Merstham theory cropped up.

"Having accepted the theory that Lestrange was hiding, but that his enemy had found him out, I naturally wondered how the enemy had succeeded in penetrating the secret, and the hypothesis I hit on to explain that situation can be applied to the Merstham theory. Lestrange probably gave away his identity unconsciously in one of his books. He may have written some description or some anecdote which to his own brother, or to any other intimate, gave away the secret of the writer's identity. Employing our new Merstham theory, can't you imagine Edward reading one of Lestrange's books—say *The Charterhouse Case*, and saying to himself 'James, my boy, I've got you! You've given yourself away this time and you're for it!'"

"Yes. Yes. That's quite good reasoning," admitted Vargon. "If your hypothesis is right, you ought to get a lead from the publishers, because they're the only people who knew where Lestrange lived."

"Not quite," replied Warner. "There's Miss Clarke, Lestrange's bankers, and the postmen. Vivian Lestrange is a striking name, and anyone of the sorters or postmen might have said to their acquaintances 'That writer chap lives at Temple Grove. Funny that no one ever sees him.'…"

"Detecting must resolve itself into one vast mark of inter-rogation," chuckled Vargon. "You go from pillar to post asking interminable questions, and eliminating one theory after another until you're left with the only tenable one. If truth resides at the bottom of a well, you have a lot of pumping to do before you uncover it."

"Detecting consists of asking the right questions," replied Warner. "Just as a barrister proves his case by examination and cross-examination, so does the detective, and one of the most important people he has to examine is himself. Asking myself questions is my chief way of forming theories, and when I have formed one, I seek to demolish it with more questions. For instance, I can ask myself this: 'If Lestrange was killed in Hampstead, how was his body conveyed to Kirkham?' The answer is 'in a car' undoubtedly. One can conjure up the idea of the murderer arriving at Temple Grove in a car, being admitted by either Mrs. Fife or Lestrange himself, going into the study and shooting his man. What does he do then? Takes the body and puts it into the car and drives away with it. But from our observations at Kirkham Barns we have assumed that two people were necessary to get the body up from the river to the cottage. Query. Did Mrs. Fife accompany the murderer in the car as soon as the murder was accomplished? The answer to that is 'No.' Someone stayed behind in Temple Grove to clean and polish the house and to remove all possible traces of the occupants. To cut a long story short I'm inclining to the theory that Lestrange was killed on Saturday night, but that Mrs. Fife and the murderer stayed in the house over the Sunday, polishing, scrubbing, and removing evidence, and that they set out together on Sunday night."

"The housekeeper seems to me to be a bit of a problem," argued Vargon. "To put the matter at its baldest, can you see the murderer shooting his man in cold blood and then saying to the housekeeper, 'Here, see what I've done. How much do you want to keep quiet?' I'd suggest a few alterations to that. First, Mrs. Fife, being a bad lot all round, routs out Lestrange's secret and sells it to the problematical enemy and later takes blood money to keep a still tongue. Second,—and a more probable alternative,—she finds Lestrange's body when she enters the house on Sunday and loses her head and does a bolt lest she be accused of killing her employer."

"Since I'm assuming that Mrs. Fife lived at Temple Grove, the second line of reasoning doesn't appeal to me," replied Warner. "The first may be somewhere near the truth."

"And now for another question which has been at the back of my mind ever since we propounded the Merstham theory," said Vargon. "Don't you think it's a bit improbable that if Edward Merstham killed his brother, he'd have brought his body back to the very district where their story was known? Damn it all! Wouldn't every instinct of caution have bidden him keep away from the locality where he was known?"

"The facts disagree with your argument," retorted Warner. "Kirkham Barns is so situated that no one would come across it by chance when they were looking for a suitable place to park a corpse. That cottage was deliberately chosen for its purpose by someone who knew it well, and by someone who had means of knowing that Sir Duncan Grant was abroad. You can't have the argument both ways: either you say 'the place was chosen by chance'—and that is ridiculous, or else you admit that 'the place was chosen by someone who knew it well,' in which case they took the risk which you have just described. Personally I favour the theory that there was method in the choice, and that inevitably leads me to another question. Did Sir Duncan Grant know the Mersthams?"

Vargon's shaggy brows drew together over his deep-set eyes.

"I think he probably did," he replied. "I told you they were keen fishermen and they fished in his waters as likely as not.

You're suggesting that the murderer had the pretty notion of handing old Grant the baby to hold?"

"It's a theory," replied Warner. "In the nature of things, if the cottage hadn't burnt out, that corpse wouldn't have been found until Grant came to spend another week-end at Kirkham. Judging by the way things were arranged, I'm of the opinion that the burning of the cottage was accidental rather than intentional. The great idea was to confine the fire to the fireplace, in which case the body might not have been found for months."

Warner sat up and threw away the end of his cigar.

"You have given me a workable theory," he said, "and I'm uncommonly grateful. I'll look into the career of Edward Merstham and see if we can come to any conclusions. Many thanks for the talk—you've set my mind humming with ideas."

The older man laughed.

"I've got a notion that you've kept your choicest ideas to yourself throughout. For all I know you may be wondering if I disposed of Lestrange myself."

Warner laughed. "Sorry to have given you such a bad impression of my mental processes. My own idea's a bit wild, but not quite so wild as that. I'll try it out on you if I think it's worthy to be put into words."

"That's right. Try it on the dog," growled Vargon. "Good night. Good night. Don't go woolgathering over old Duncan Grant."

CHAPTER VIII

W HEN CHIEF INSPECTOR WARNER RETURNED TO LONDON, he found Bond waiting for him when he reached Scotland Yard.

"Cheer up, Bond!" said Warner. "That corpse is a perfectly good corpse, and just the article you've been wanting for days past. Moreover it's hallmarked; it was carrying Vivian Lestrange's pocket-book about with it."

"What's that, sir?" demanded Bond. "I thought they said that the body was burned past recognition? Was the chap kind enough to leave his pocket-book on the table before he settled down in the chimney space?"

"Don't be so jaundiced over it," replied Warner cheerfully. "I've never known a man who's so hard to please. The pocket-book was undoubtedly meant to be demolished by the flames, only, as you know and as I know, fires play odd tricks. You can put a book on a bonfire, but unless you do a little good work with a poker, the book won't burn through! What happened in this case was that the leather binding charred through and made a tough ashy surround to the close-packed pages inside. There are a couple of pages left in which the handwriting is not only recognisable but decipherable. Have a look at these."

Warner handed the other man the photographs which had been taken of the innermost leaves of the charred pocket-book, and Bond studied them at length.

"Yes," he said. "It's the same writing,—and these notes correspond to the subject matter of the manuscript at Temple Grove."

"And that means we're on firm ground at last," said Warner. "Previously to this we could toy with various ideas, including your original theory that the whole yarn was a mare's nest—another invention from the fertile mind of a best seller. Now, whatever the eventual explanation of the facts proves to be, we know that we are dealing with a case of murder, and we've got to get down to it. Now here's the outline of some facts I culled from a lawyer in Ross."

Bond listened to the other's narrative with thoughtful face but when he came to the close of his story, Warner said,

"That's all hypothetical, of course, though it seems a likely line to follow up. And now tell me your news. I could tell from the look of you that you'd got a story up your sleeve. Has the thoughtful Miss Clarke contrived a vanishing trick on her own account, or provided you with a perfectly fresh problem to keep you awake o' nights?"

Bond grinned. "You're a good guesser, sir," he replied. "I've got some news, although it's news to me that I spread my ideas all over my face. Here's another of Miss Clarke's little stories. Apparently she rang up here yesterday and asked for you, and they didn't consider it politic to tell her that you were out of London, so they said her message should be given to you when you came in, and meanwhile when would she be at home? The upshot of it was that I called in to see her yesterday evening, and after a few pointed remarks regretting that you hadn't time to deal with the matter yourself, she produced a small parcel and asked me to have a look at it. It was a neatly done up affair, not too large to slip into a good sized post-box, and although Miss

Clarke had cut the string and examined the contents, she'd kept the whole thing intact otherwise,—packing paper and all. Inside was a typewritten letter and two neat packets of £1 Treasury notes, packed between cardboards. The notes were in sequence, four hundred of them. Perhaps you'd like to do a spot more guessing?"

Warner laughed aloud. "The Treasury notes were those that the bank paid out when they cashed Lestrange's last cheque? Tell me more, Bond... This is damned interesting."

"It's a damned funny story, sir!" cried Bond, exasperation creeping into his voice again. "I'm not satisfied about that young woman, she's too jolly sure of herself! Here's the typewritten letter that was in the packet. The finger-print people have been over it."

"And the only prints on it are those of Miss Clarke herself? Your face is more informative than you'd believe, Bond!"

Warner took the slip of paper and read,

"The enclosed notes are in payment of a debt contracted to your mother many years ago. With every good wish from the sender."

"But how nice!" said Warner. "That sort of thing never happens to me! What do you make of it?"

Bond shrugged his shoulders. "Somebody's being funny!" he growled, "but there's a neatness in their technique, I admit. Miss Clarke was very helpful. She took the trouble to point out that the cardboards which packed the notes were the same variety as the cardboard you get at Woolworth's behind their packets of manuscript paper. She was quite right, too, it's the same stuff all right. The packing paper can be bought there, too. The address was typed on a slip which was neatly pasted on to the wrapping paper. The postmark was E.C.1, and the packet was posted at the General Post Office some time between six-thirty and seven-thirty the night before last,—just dropped ready stamped into the letter-box, not handed over the counter. There's not a thing to get hold of to enable you to prove anything."

"This story has quite a lot in common with the whole case," said Warner. "It's susceptible to various interpretations. For instance, you have a half-formed assumption brewing in your mind that Miss Clarke appropriated the notes on a previous occasion, posted them to herself and then informed us of their arrival with the expression of the world's most surprised woman. What reason did she give for informing you of this gift from the unknown?"

"Miss Clarke is an exceedingly clear-headed young woman," replied Bond. "I may find her irritating,—I admit that I do, but I don't under-estimate her ability. Her explanation for telling us about the arrival of the packet was thoroughly sensible. She said that the whole thing was incomprehensible to her, that so far as she knew, no one had ever owed her mother four hundred pounds, and that considering the abnormal events of the past ten days she considered it wiser to tell the police immediately anything unusual happened to her. She admitted quite frankly that she was frightened. She didn't know who sent the notes, or why they were sent and she would rather that we took charge of them."

"Comprehensively on the side of the angels, in fact," commented Warner. "If the young woman is involved in any part of this crime,—which up to the present, I have not believed,—I can foresee that we shall have a busy time getting even with her. She is, as you say, admirably clear-headed, and she can see more than one step in front of her. Bearing that in mind, what could have been her motive in posting those notes to herself and then telling us about them? If she took them from Temple Grove, or even if Lestrange gave them to her, she would have known that their numbers would be in our possession. She couldn't have changed them herself."

"No, that's as clear as daylight," agreed Bond, "but meantime, what is the legal position? If a sum of money is sent to you through the post, isn't it legally yours? It's not as though we have any proof that those notes were stolen from Lestrange. We may believe that they were, but we have no actual proof that he didn't hand them over to someone before his death."

"H'm... It's a nice point," said Warner. "Meantime Miss Clarke has done the most sensible thing she could have in handing them over to our care. We're faced with another of these 'either or' problems which are so irritating to your logical mind. On the one side, if we assume that Miss Clarke posted these notes to herself it seems probable that she is implicated all through the crime. That pocket-book has proved to us that the murdered man was connected with Temple Grove, and it's obviously on the cards that Miss Clarke has knowledge of the crime. In that case she is working with an accomplice, because she could not have conveyed a body from Temple Grove to Kirkham by herself... Well, what's the objection? I should have thought even your sceptical mind would have agreed to those statements."

Bond had wrinkled up his brow into a frown of thoughtfulness and he spoke slowly when he replied, like a man groping his way.

"I'm not good at putting my thoughts into words as you are, sir, but I've been plugging away at this story, trying to make sense of it. I never did cotton to this yarn about an invisible author. It seems to me too tall a story altogether... You say we're faced with an 'either or,' and, to my mind, the alternatives boil down to this. Either Miss Clarke is telling the truth or else she isn't."

"Yes," agreed Warner, "and then?"

"And then," continued Bond, "I'd say if she isn't telling the whole truth, it's no use counting on a single word she says. We've two possibilities. A. She's told the truth. B. She hasn't. In B. case I'm not willing to believe that any man ever lived at Temple Grove, or that Vivian Lestrange is anybody but Eleanor Clarke herself."

"Agreed,—and who is your corpse?"

"I don't know, but I'd hazard an opinion that it was some man whom Miss Clarke had planned to dispose of, and she—with the brain that planned *The Charterhouse Case*—"

"Ah! you've read it," put in Warner.

"Yes, I've read it, and I give it top marks... The brain that planned that book would be capable of thinking out any scheme. The man who was killed and whose body was found at Kirkham need never have been in London at all. Maybe he was killed somewhere in the locality where the body was found, and that pocket-book was put with the remains simply to throw dust in our eyes."

With narrowed eyes and knitted brows, Bond unfolded his argument, his voice gaining confidence and his words coming more easily as he developed his theme.

"Think of the ingenuity of it!" he said. "To anyone who had the patience and the brains to carry it through, the scheme must have looked almost fool proof! Assume that this young woman was determined to kill some man who had defrauded her. She doesn't go at it hammer and tongs, all in a rage, and get herself hanged as the result. She bides her time and builds up the mythical identity of Vivian Lestrange. Obviously Mrs. Fife was in the plot with her, and together they planned this scheme and chose their time for it.

"The victim was killed and his body disposed of in the cottage and rendered unrecognisable in the process, and then came the brilliant idea of leaving just enough evidence with the corpse to convince us that the whole story hung together. Why, it's a master stroke, sir!" cried Bond. "The idea of most clever murderers is to conceal the identity of their victim, but this goes one better. There's a ready made identity for the victim,—and how we're ever going to get past it, and slip the young woman up, I don't see."

"Go up to the top of the class!" said Warner. "I apologise, Bond. I put you down for a first-class routine worker, never guessing you'd the imagination of Wilkie Collins."

"I am a routine worker, sir, and I'm not ashamed of it," said Bond, his lean face flushing. "I'm the last person to invent fantastic explanations for straightforward cases, but this case isn't straightforward; it's wheels within wheels. Once you admit that Miss Clarke's story may be the invention of a fertile mind, you're faced with the most fantastic possibilities,—and the explanation I've put forward accounts for the facts."

"It certainly does," said Warner. "Don't think I'm belittling your mental processes. Far from it. I'd say you'd done some very sound thinking,—but you've only dealt with alternative B—that Miss Clarke has been lying throughout. To create a balance, I am going to argue on the lines of alternative A, that she has told the truth."

"And how the deuce we're ever going to get evidence to prove it, I can't see," groaned Bond. "Sorry, sir. That young woman has got on my nerves."

"Simply because she is a type that has not previously come under your observation," said Warner. "You have a tidy mind, and you like to card-index the characters you meet.

"You know the womanly woman, the obvious bad lot, the shop-lifting type, and the hardened harridan, always drunk of an evening. Miss Clarke is a bit of a blue-stocking, the modern intellectual who meets a man on equal terms and admits not his superiority—nor yet panders to it. You're irritated because you can't place her in your experience that's all... Now for alternative A.

"Vivian Lestrange was killed at Temple Grove, and his body put into a car and eventually conveyed to Kirkham. We have got to do some intensive research on the subject of cars seen near Temple Grove on Saturday or Sunday nights. One of the questions that arises is this. Granted that Mrs. Fife was an accessory to the murder, why didn't she ring up Miss Clarke and tell her not to come to Temple Grove for a few days? It seems to me that the criminals were so sure of their secret that they didn't care a damn how soon the absence of Lestrange became known; also they were satisfied that nothing Miss Clarke could tell would be of any danger to them. Those points want careful thinking out. Then comes the story of this little parcel with Lestrange's pound notes in it. That looks as though the criminals were trying to implicate Miss Clarke. Remember that nothing has been published so far concerning this story. I am pretty certain that if a murder was committed at Temple Grove, the murderers did not hang about outside the house watching to see what happened next. They would have made themselves scarce and waited to learn developments from the newspapers. Now it's not every secretary who would have had the common sense to act as promptly as Miss Clarke did. Suppose that she had not informed the police immediately. You would have learned eventually from the tradespeople—or from one of your point duty men—that Temple Grove seemed uninhabited, although neither newspapers nor milk had been counter-ordered. You would have found Miss Clarke—and things would have looked very fishy for her. If in addition, she was caught trying to change notes which had been paid out for Vivian Lestrange's cheque, she would have looked fishier still. I think that the murderers hoped that Miss Clarke would provide the red herring. Now we have both stated our case, and it's no use arguing the alternatives any further until we have more evidence. Publicity is the next thing. We have avoided it up till now, because we had at first no definite evidence that a crime had been committed. Tomorrow, the morning papers are going to be simply plastered with Vivian Lestrange."

"I'm glad that the ensuing correspondence will be dealt with by your department, sir," said Bond with his saturnine grin. "I can imagine the sort of thing you'll get."

"Don't you worry about that," retorted Warner. "You're going to have plenty to do to keep you occupied. Up till now, we haven't bothered much about the neighbours at Temple Grove.

"We have learnt that Mr. and Mrs. Mallings, who live on the one side, have been away on the Continent for a fortnight, and that Lee Vernon was away from his studio during the week-end of Lestrange's disappearance. You've got to check up those facts, and to badger both parties to tell you every detail they've ever noticed about the occupants of Temple Grove. Hang it all, even in London, you're bound to notice that you've got neighbours. Human nature's the same all the world over. People may say 'I don't know anything about them' but they manage to notice a lot all the same."

"Temple Grove must have been an ideal setting for this particular crime," said Bond. "There are only two lots of neighbours, all told. The Mallings, on the one side of Temple Grove, have only lived there for six months and they're frequently away. The previous tenant of their house is dead. Then on the further side is Lee Vernon's studio. Lee Vernon may be a good painter, I believe he is, but he's as blind as a bat so far as his neighbours are concerned. The house opposite with the long garden which stretched right down to the end of the cul-de-sac is up for sale. The house-agents call it 'this secluded residence' and, my hat! for once they're telling the truth. That road was fairly laid out for people with secrets to keep!"

"Well, you go and rout out their secrets!" admonished Warner. "It's no use looking at me with a sceptical eye any longer; you'd a certain amount of excuse while we were corpseless, but now the genuine article's provided you might at least look as though your heart was in the job! That corpse is going to be christened Vivian Lestrange pro tem, and don't you forget it!

"And now, just to cheer you up, I might tell you of another little notion that I've been toying with. You have heard what Langston's had to say,—how they first met Miss Clarke and accepted her as Vivian Lestrange and how Marriott persuaded her to come to a little dinner party."

"Yes, sir," agreed Bond, "to meet Michael Ashe."

"Exactly. To meet Michael Ashe," and Warner looked at the other man with a little smile deepening the fine wrinkles round his misleadingly ingenuous eyes.

"Where does Ashe come into it?" demanded Bond.

"That's just the question which I've been amusing myself with!" replied Warner. "Ashe deliberately approached Marriott with the request that he should meet Vivian Lestrange. Now lots of other people have pestered Langston's for news of Vivian Lestrange, but the enquiries generally came either from journalists, reviewers, or the news agencies which like to collect gossip about well-known writers. Ashe is in a different category; he wanted to meet a fellow author, but behind his request there was human curiosity, and when he met our intelligent secretary he was simply staggered—so Marriott told me."

"Have you seen him yet, sir,—Ashe, I mean?"

"No. The great idea only recently occurred to me. If Marriott's right, Ashe got near Lestrange's secret. Miss Clarke played her part so well that Ashe was made to look merely boorish in his assumption that Vivian Lestrange must be a man. Also, Miss Clarke left Marriott's flat and went home in a taxi, some little while before Ashe himself left. He had offered to see her home, but his offer was refused."

Warner paused here and lit a cigarette, holding out his case to Bond.

"If you were placed in the same circumstances, Bond, and had wanted very much to find out where Miss Clarke lived, what would you have done about it?"

"Speaking officially, sir?" demanded Bond.

"No. Unofficially."

"Humph. Not so easy. You could advertise for the taxi man."

"Yes, and give the show away to the lady. That's the worst of advertisements, they're a two-edged weapon. No. If I had been in Michael Ashe's place, and the devil of curiosity was really roused in my breast concerning that remarkable young woman, I should have argued thus. Miss Clarke left in a taxi. Ergo, the taxi was called up from a convenient rank. On leaving Marriott's flat, I should have ascertained from either the servants or the porter which rank was the nearest in order to call a taxi for myself. I should then have made straight for the rank and offered a reward to the man who found me the taxi driver who went to pick up a fare at Melrose Mansions at eleven o'clock that evening. When I'd found the driver I should have given him a good tip in exchange for the address to which he'd driven the lady that night,—she might have dropped a brooch or bracelet which I was anxious to return. And once, oh unbelieving Bond, I had found Eleanor Clarke's address, I should have had very little difficulty in locating her employer."

Bond listened with his intent frown.

"What's the connection between Michael Ashe and the Merstham brothers, sir?" he enquired.

Warner spread out his hands in a gesture of uncertainty. "Who knows?" he replied. "Maybe both theories are utterly wide of the mark. I'm not yet convinced that anything which either of us has suggested this evening is likely to be the truth, but when one's absolutely at sea, any mark is better to steer by than none. I'm merely indicating lines of research. Anyway let us sum up. Suggestion one, is yours,—and it's neat, ingenious, and workmanlike—to wit: Vivian Lestrange is Eleanor Clarke, and the dead man is unknown to us,—he may be any of the few hundred million males on this earth, in which case, every clue we have found is a false clue and leads us nowhere. Pray heaven you're wrong! Suggestion two, comes via our friend Mr. Vargon. Vivian Lestrange was the pen name of James Merstham, and he was killed by his brother Edward. Suggestion three, is purely circumstantial, being that Michael Ashe showed a marked desire to meet Vivian Lestrange in the flesh and was put off with the understudy. All these suggestions are independent and destructive of one another. Now for positive evidence. We have a corpse in one place, specimens of handwriting in another—this links up Kirkham and Temple Grove. We have also notes to the value of four hundred pounds cashed by Lestrange's cheque and received through the post by Miss Eleanor Clarke... By the way any concrete evidence concerning the decease of the late Mrs. Clarke?"

Bond suddenly grinned. "Yes, I thought of that, sir. Mother and daughter, what? Our Miss Clarke and the unknown Mrs. Fife. Nothing doing. Death certificate all in order."

"Well, well. These bright ideas are so soon demolished by our elaborate system of state registration," sighed Warner. "For you, Bond, is a week of toil with the neighbours of Temple Grove and the private life of Miss Eleanor Clarke. For me, spade work into the peculiarities of ex-convict Merstham, the whereabouts of Mr. Michael Ashe, and the possibilities of suborning taxi drivers."

"Yes, sir," said Bond submissively, "and if at the end of the week of toil you've mentioned, I have proved that no man lived at Temple Grove, and you have proved that ex-convict Merstham is dead, that Michael Ashe is in South Africa, and that no taxi driver ever received any enquiries about fares from Melrose Mansions, what do we do then?"

"My dear Bond! Guess again! guess again!" replied Warner, though that as he knew, was not the answer which Bond had hoped for.

CHAPTER IX

WHEN CHIEF INSPECTOR WARNER CALLED ON MR. Marriott at his office the next morning, he found the publisher looking as exasperated as a man can be. Warner smiled down pleasantly at the older man, observing the pile of newspapers which lay tossed on the floor by Marriott's desk.

"Good morning, sir. I should think your advertisement department must be sitting back and smiling happily. The Press seems to have done you well,—notices highly eulogistic in fact."

Marriott's face was a study. "I have been in the publishing business for thirty years," he replied, "and this is the first occasion when I have regretted the fact. Advertisement! My dear Inspector, the whole thing is simply nauseating! I believe in advertising books on their merits, but for this firm to be made the target for the cheapest form of notoriety, to be plastered across every contemptible rag, to be mobbed by every Tom, Dick and Harry from the gutters of every provincial Fleet Street…" Having tied himself into an inextricable knot of clauses, Marriott gave up his sentence in despair and thumped the desk with a clenched fist. "I am a reticent and decent-minded man," he groaned, "and this orgy of sensationalism is nothing less than revolting to me!"

"Oh, come, don't feel so bitter over it," said Warner. "The printers will have to work overtime getting out new impressions of Lestrange's works to meet the demands of a voracious public… besides, you know, we were very careful to safeguard your dignity. You've noticed that there is no mention of the fact that Langston's accepted Miss Eleanor Clarke as the author of *The Charterhouse Case*."

Marriott's face flushed, but he replied with dignity.

"That was thoughtful of you, Chief Inspector. The whole story is a mystery which it is beyond my power to fathom, but I'm not going to admit that I was a fool, even though I've been made a fool of—handsomely! I still abide by my previous opinion,—that nowadays you can't tell a man's writings from a woman's. We have a bias—I acknowledge it—a tendency to regard any powerful and thoughtful piece of writing as emanating from a man's mind. We took it for granted that Lestrange was a man, until that remarkable young woman came here and made hay of all our theories…" Marriott leaned back in his chair and looked thoughtfully at the bookcase opposite to him. "I was born in 1874," he said, apparently irrelevantly. "I have seen three eras, the Victorian, the Edwardian and the post-war, and I'll tell you this. There is hardly a single conception of my youth which hasn't had to be modified to fit the manners of today. Women! In my youth, there were two categories, the virtuous and the non-virtuous. The first knew very little about men; in a woman's presence we ordered our speech, our manners, our actions, to suit certain conventions. We didn't swear, we didn't get drunk, we didn't discuss our mistresses in the society of women. Nowadays the girls swear as much as the men, they claim the same moral licence,—yes, and you read of an Oxford don deploring the fact that he lived to see a woman undergraduate drunk at a Commemoration ball."

Seeing Warner's expression, Marriott added, "What has all this to do with your case? A lot, my dear Inspector! You say to me with a smile on your face—'Fancy you being had like that!' Damn it! I know what I'm talking about! There isn't a compartment of a man's mind that the modern woman hasn't explored. She knows the violence of his speech and passions, she writes of both. I could show you the manuscripts written by girls of today that would make your hair rise on your scalp! The cunningest murder stories are planned by women's brains. If Miss Dorothy Sayers had chosen to write under the name of Jack Johnson, would you have guessed the writer was a woman? Consider another category.—Take Tennyson Jesse. Have you read *Tom Fool*? Would you have said that was a woman's writing? If you'd read *Red Wagon* would you have said, 'ah, yes—a woman'? if the name on the title page hadn't told you who'd written it? I'll tell you what,—I'll lend you three new books, and if at the end of a week you can tell me the sex of the writers correctly, I'll send ten pounds to any charity you like to name. There's no criterion nowadays; women have claimed equality with men, and apart from the very front rank of genius they make good their claim."

"Really, you're most upsetting," complained Warner. "All through this case I have been holding on—like a drowning man—to the belief that Vivian Lestrange was a man. I've believed what Miss Clarke said, pluming myself on my ability to detect a liar and now you've gone over to the enemy. You're like Bond, who says that Eleanor Clarke and Vivian Lestrange are one and the same, and the identity of Vivian Lestrange was created to provide an identity for a corpse."

"Bond sounds a sensible man to me," growled Marriott. "If you'd heard that young woman talking Michael Ashe out of countenance, you'd have believed her capable of anything!"

Suddenly Marriott was consumed by mirth; he lay back in his chair and laughed till he shook.

"Was your mother a congenital defective and your grandmother a moron?" he quoted. "My God! I thought she was going to ask him if his origin was explained by parthenogenesis! It was pretty near the ham bone, I'll tell you that!"

"Sorry I wasn't there!" said Warner regretfully. "I should have loved it. Funnily enough, you've butted right into the subject which I wanted to discuss with you."

"What? Virgin birth?" demanded Marriott amazedly.

"My God, no!" said Warner, and suddenly both men began to laugh again.

"Neither biology nor miracles for me," said the Chief Inspector. "I want to talk about Michael Ashe."

"God bless my soul! What the deuce for?" demanded Marriott. "He's not a woman, is he? I must have something to hold on to, for sanity's sake. I'm not willing to give a definite and incontrovertible answer concerning the sex of a writer as displayed in his or her writing, but Michael Ashe is himself all right."

"Thank heaven for small comforts," said Warner. "When one's case resembles a mass of shifting sand, one is thankful for stability of any kind. The point I want to discuss is this. When Ashe said that he wanted to meet Lestrange, do you think there could have been an ulterior motive in his mind? It has occurred to me that though a writer may conceal his identity under a pen name, and his person behind a ten foot wall, yet he may unconsciously shout his identity aloud through the medium of his writing. Assuming—as I still do—that Vivian Lestrange was a man with a motive for concealing himself from his enemies, may he not have written something which an acquaintance or a relation could recognise, saying, 'only so and so could have written that'?"

"Look here," said Marriott, "you may be pleased with this little idea of yours. No doubt it seems to you a very pretty idea. You're suggesting that Lestrange being dead, you're going to do your best to hang Ashe for it. Kindly remember that I am a publisher and the two names you're chattering about so blithely have been the most important names on Langston's list for the past three years. Don't expect me to join in your little enthusiasms, that's all. God bless my soul! You will be suggesting that Bailley and I killed Lestrange next!"

"I'm in the state of mind when I'm willing to consider any and every suggestion," replied Warner mildly. "If I could fit you and your partner out with motives, I'd suspect you with pleasure,—but you don't really make sense as suspects, you know. So far as I can make out, you have both lived the most immaculate lives, and it was all to your interests to keep Lestrange alive. Of course, it might be argued that you'd engineered an almighty fine advertisement, but I still believe that Lestrange alive is more profitable to you than Lestrange dead... That's all by the way. Now forget all about your natural reluctance to discuss your authors and tell me what you know of Michael Ashe."

Marriott sat with his shoulders hunched up almost to his ears, a perfect picture of depression.

"It's a fantastic idea," he grumbled to himself, "but there's no getting away from it that Ashe was simply staggered when I introduced him to Miss Lestrange—or Miss Clarke—or whatever she chooses to call herself. I remember Ashe's face when he said 'but it's impossible!' Devil take it! What a situation!"

"Yes, it has its dramatic side," agreed Warner. "When did you first meet Ashe?"

"Personally? Oh, not much more than a couple of years ago. You remember that first book of his, *Trade Winds*? It was posted to us from South America, with a covering letter saying the author was travelling and had no fixed address, and that he'd write to us later; meanwhile would we hold the typescript whether we accepted it or not. We heard again a month later,— from a hotel at Bristol, I think it was, and the contract was signed by post. We didn't meet Ashe till six months later... Have you ever come across him?"

"No. I've read his books though. Jolly fine stuff, too. He knows his subject; no one ever wrote that description of Tierra without having seen it."

"No. You're right there... I should say that Ashe is about fifty years of age; he is a big fellow nearly six feet; with slightly grizzled fair hair. One of the Norse type, with a long head, prominent nose and powerful jaw; he's got curious blue eyes, very deeply set, eyes that seem to smoulder like a flame when he's out of temper. He's a noticeable fellow, not one you could easily forget either. I remember I wasn't any too happy at that little party of mine. He looked at that girl like a blood horse might look at a mare... He remembered his manners, but his eyes looked hot."

"I think a few words with Master Ashe might be interesting," said Warner meditatively. "There's just a chance that he might know something... That's the whole point in this enquiry. We've got to find out the identity of the individual who hid behind the name of Vivian Lestrange. Until we discover that we shan't get anywhere. Where does Ashe live?"

Marriott stretched out his hands again in that gesture of hopelessness. "The deuce knows," he said. "He doesn't live anywhere. He's a nomad. When the mood takes him, he'll stay at the Savoy; then he goes off for a night or two to a sailors' doss house in Deptford, then up to Liverpool, maybe at the Adelphi, maybe down in the docks. We write to him at his club—the Addison, in John Street, and just wait for an answer till he chooses to write. He's generally on hand when there's proof reading to be done, but he's just finished the proofs of his new novel and gone off, the Lord knows where. He talked about spending the spring in Majorca. Quite as likely as not he's gone to Bangkok or Greenland or Tanganyika. There's no saying where he'll go when the mood takes him, and there aren't many quarters of the globe he hasn't wandered in, in his time. I remember saying to him... Good heavens! you'll be using that against him next! It's time I got on with my proper work!"

"Out with it!" said Warner. "You're not the man to sit tight with an uneasy conscience. You'd better unburden it, and then you can get back to your job with a peaceful mind."

Marriott sighed. "This sort of situation isn't to my liking at all," he groaned. "I've just remembered that when Ashe first talked to me of Lestrange, he mentioned the Dartmoor chapters in *The Charterhouse Case* and said that it seemed to him that the man who wrote them must have been in prison himself to be able to describe it like that."

"Nothing much in that," said Warner. "It's the sort of thing anybody might have said. In fact it makes my idea less probable because if Ashe had recognised Lestrange's identity through one of his books, I don't think he'd have made that particular remark to stick in your memory. Well, here are our facts:—Michael

Ashe has only been known to you for three years—since the publication of *Trade Winds*. You don't know his address and you're willing to hazard anywhere on the globe for his present whereabouts. Only a few more questions. When did you see him last?"

"A month ago," replied Marriott.

"And can you give me a photograph of him?"

"No, I can't, he wouldn't have one published."

"H-m… resembled Lestrange there," said Warner. "Well, I'll get on with some more of my wild notions. By the way, do you mind telling me your full address, and the taxi rank which is most convenient when any of your departing guests wants a taxi?"

Marriott looked at him mournfully. "I live at 27 Melrose Mansions, Bloomsbury," he replied, "and the nearest cab rank is at the corner of Gower Street."

"And what was the date of your little party, when you introduced the sceptical Ashe to the mysterious Lestrange?"

Marriott took a diary out of his pocket and studied it. "February 14th," he replied.

"How appropriate," murmured Warner. "Well, I know you're anxious to get rid of me. Cheer up! Perhaps all our theories are wrong and Vivian Lestrange is taking a well deserved holiday in the south of France, his letter of explanation to Miss Clarke being lost in the post and Michael Ashe is sunning himself at Antibes."

"And that corpse?" enquired Marriott.

"A mere burglar who pinched Lestrange's pocket-book when he burgled Temple Grove," said Warner cheerfully.

"Go away," said Marriott. "You tire me."

Leaving the publishers Warner made his way to the corner of Gower Street, where he found a seedy looking old man answering the telephone which was fixed up for the purpose of summoning taxis.

"Are you generally on duty here?" demanded Warner.

"Dooty? Well, I dunno as 'ow I'd call it that," wheezed the ancient, smiling knowingly at Warner out of his humorous old eyes. "Dooty! That reminds me o' a catechism which we larned when I was young. Me dooty towards me neighbour... 'Ow does it go? To do unto all men as I would they do unto me."

"Not a bad idea, that," said Warner, feeling in his pocket and producing a shilling.

"Thank 'ee, sir. Thank 'ee kindly," beamed the old man. "Not that I'm what you'd call a perfeshional, an amacher I am, but then it suits them," pointing with a thumb towards the taxi rank, "and now and agen it soots me. And what can I do fer you, sir?"

"I'm looking for a taxi driver who was on this rank about eleven o'clock in the evening on February 14th last," said Warner.

"St. Valentine's day, that'd be, sir. Not that yer ever sees a Valentine these days, but I tell you what. I won a bit on a dog that day and the dog was called Valentine. Something in it, I sez. Well, as it 'appens, yer 'umble was 'ere that night. Ever read Dickens, sir?"

"Yes. Uriah Heep," said Warner, almost automatically. "If you were here on St. Valentine's evening, can you tell me anything else that happened to fix it in your mind?"

"That I can! That I can!" chuckled the old man. "Another bit o' fat that was for yer 'umble. A big chap now,—as big as yourself, and a real toff—'e came along to know 'oo answered a call to Melrose Mansions about 'alf an hour before 'e came along 'isself. Now it was Joe Bates took 'is cab along fer that job, as I did know, seein' as 'ow I'd given 'im the haddress meself."

"And then?" asked Warner, clinking the coins in his pockets.

"Well, the toff wanted Joe Bates's haddress,—and a bit of fat it was fer 'im too. Seemed a lidy 'ad dropped 'er pearls at a party, an' the toff, 'e wanted to give 'em back to 'er. May be 'e did, may be 'e didn't," continued the ancient thoughtfully, "and Joe, 'e says to me 'I only told 'im the block o' flats I dropped 'er at, there weren't no 'arm in that.' Though you never can tell now, you never can tell," he rumbled on, "but these gels nowadays, you never know, you never know… Still, the toff, 'e paid up like a gent."

"Well, you'd better give me Joe Bates's address," said Warner, producing another shilling, and the old man's eyes fairly gleamed.

"That I will an' welcome," he said, "but seein' as that's Joe 'imself, sittin' in his keb at the back of the rank—"

"Then he's the chap for me, grandfather," said Warner cheerfully and the old man touched his cap. "Good luck to 'ee, young gen'leman!" he wheezed. "I bin a crossin' sweeper, an' a pavement artist in me time, an' onst I used to run alongside them growlers to lend an 'and with trunks, but I never 'ad a better bit o' fat in me life than wot came along 'ere St. Valentine. Ten bob I made that day, as I'm an honest man, an' I was that drunk next day, drunk as a lord I was…"

Warner learned from Joe Bates, the taxi driver, just exactly what he had expected to learn. Shortly after eleven p.m. on February 14th (remembered by the taxi drivers as the day on which "old Jarge" won a bit on the dogs), a telephone call had summoned a taxi to Melrose Mansions. Joe Bates had taken his cab round and picked up his fare,—a young lady in an evening cloak whom he had driven to Clare Court, Hampstead. When the taxi driver returned to his home in St. Pancras, shortly after midnight, he had found a car waiting outside the building where he lived and a man sitting at the driving wheel had called to him and asked him if his name were Bates. After some discussion, the taxi driver had told his interlocutor that he had driven the lady from Melrose Mansions to Clare Court.

Warner left the taxi rank and walked back along Gower Street with a troubled face. His guess had been a good one; Michael Ashe, devoured by curiosity about Vivian Lestrange, had simply taken the most obvious means of finding out where she lived,—a process that was very easy to anybody who used their wits. After that, Ashe had doubtless watched outside Clare Court the next morning until the lady of the dinner party came out and then followed her to Temple Grove. And then? Warner tried to think what he would himself have done, impelled by a similar curiosity. By means of watching for several days Ashe could easily have come to the right conclusion, granting that he had his own suspicions as to the identity of Vivian Lestrange. After that, everything was wild surmise. Warner felt that a few more words with Eleanor Clarke were indicated to help him to arrange his ideas.

A telephone call to Clare Court told the Chief Inspector that Eleanor Clarke would be at home immediately after lunch, so having first fortified himself with a meal, Warner made his way to Hampstead.

Miss Clarke's greeting was wholehearted.

"Oh! I'm so glad to see you," she said, with relief in her voice. "Life is simply night-mareish, and every time the post comes I'm terrified of what it will bring. Have you heard about that ridiculous parcel of notes?"

Warner laughed.

"Yes, though that isn't most people's idea of a nightmare. Still, in your case, you may well say 'Timeo Danaos.' Do you know who those notes were paid to at the bank which issued them?"

She shook her head. "I've no idea, and Inspector Bond was just surly over it, he wouldn't tell me a thing. He's a misogynist, that man. The mere sight of a woman makes him irritable. To whom do the notes belong?"

"They were paid out by the Westminster Bank for a cheque signed by Vivian Lestrange and cashed by Mrs. Fife," said Warner, watching his companion's face closely. He saw nothing but consternation in her eyes, though the colour rose hotly in her cheeks.

"Good Lord, how awful!" she groaned, then fell to thinking, her chin on her clenched hands. "That's what Bond was thinking then," she said at last. "He knew the numbers of those notes, and he supposed I had sent them to myself and then told him about it to safeguard myself... Can't you find out who sent them?" she cried, in a sudden tone of pleading, quite unlike her usual cool speech.

"I must admit that I can't see any hope of finding out at present," said Warner. "The only clue is the typescript of the note and address, and until we get farther in this case, we don't know where to look for the typewriter. You are very quick at seeing the implications behind events, Miss Clarke, and it must be obvious to you that we are doing all we can to find anyone who knew Vivian Lestrange,—who knew the man behind the name, so to speak. Obviously there was a lot of curiosity in the writing world over the identity of such a successful writer. We know that Messrs. Bailley and Marriott were anxious to meet him in the flesh. Now have you yourself ever met anyone else who expressed the same desire?"

She studied him carefully before she replied.

"No one ever asked me about Vivian Lestrange because no one knew I was employed by him. I called my employer Mr. Thomas Browne whenever I spoke of him to anybody, which wasn't often... Oh, there was Michael Ashe, of course..."

"Exactly," replied Warner, "now when did you see Mr. Ashe last?"

Obviously puzzled, she stared at Warner with knitted brows. "I only saw him that one time," she said slowly. "Why do you ask?"

Still watching her carefully, Warner replied,

"Because I have a shrewd idea that Ashe traced you to this address, and having done that he could easily have followed you to Temple Grove the next morning."

She sat very still and frowning, and when she replied, she spoke as though meditating aloud.

"I knew he didn't believe in me,—I could feel he didn't... But why, *why* should Michael Ashe have wanted to kill Mr. Lestrange? I can believe him capable of it, because he's a brute, and any sort of brutality would suit him,—but why?"

"Say, if you answer this question," said Warner softly. "Why do you assume that Mr. Lestrange is dead? What evidence have you got?"

She sat up with a start at that, but looked him straight in the face.

"I'm certain he is dead," she replied, her face white now, "I've no evidence of any kind, but the minute I saw that hole in the study window, I was certain he was dead. I'm not superstitious and I'm not a crank, but somehow I knew there was death in that room."

Warner did not reply at once, and there was a queer, strained silence in the room. At length he said.

"Intuitions of that kind are absolutely unreliable. It is only by some previous knowledge that such an idea can suggest itself to the mind. I know you had had an agitating day, debating in your mind what you ought to do about that impregnable house, but even that wasn't enough for the state of certainty you express. Are you quite sure that there wasn't some other train of thought leading up to your assumption?"

She shook her head. "No. There was nothing at all, unless you count the subconscious awareness that Temple Grove and its occupants were queer... I suppose I am getting queer in the head, too, with worrying over it all, or I shouldn't have made that idiotic statement about death in a room..."

"The thing is preying on your mind," said Warner, his voice kindly enough. "Once again, answer me as though you were on oath. Have you ever spoken to, or seen, Michael Ashe, except when you met him at Mr. Marriott's flat?"

"No. Never," she replied steadily, and then as Warner rose to go, she added:

"Do at least tell me this,—in your opinion, is Mr. Lestrange's disappearance due to murder?"

"The whole case is so obscure that it's difficult to give an answer," replied Warner, "but in my opinion, I do consider that the case I am working on, is a case of murder. I may be entirely wrong,—perhaps time will show."

CHAPTER X

A S WARNER AND BOND HAD FORESEEN, THEY WERE INUN-
dated with letters in reply to Press enquiries concerning
Vivian Lestrange; letters both signed and anonymous, thoughtful
and foolish, educated and illiterate, so that a staff of clerks was
needed to sort them out. The most frequent were from people
who stated that their own characters had been described in
Lestrange's books,—a common delusion among novel readers,
as every writer knows, but the only letter which seemed to be
of any value was an extraordinary communication addressed
to Temple Grove itself. "The Officer in Charge.—Re the late
Vivian Lestrange," ran the superscription on the envelope, and
Bond opened it with his usual expression of sceptical calm.
At the end of an hour, he was still sitting studying the neatly
typewritten sheets.

"To Whom it May Concern,
    "Vivian Lestrange is dead," began the letter. "That is
the crux of the whole affair to me, but the Press is concerning itself with another aspect of the matter. 'Who is
Vivian Lestrange?' run the black headlines of the *Mercury*.
    "'Mystery of famous author's identity,' blares the
Clarion.
    "'Have you met the author of *The Charterhouse Case*?'
demands the *Sun*—and so on.

"Here is the matter in a nutshell. The name Vivian Lestrange covers the experiences and brains of a variety of men and women. A syndicate? In some senses, yes, although the recluse of Temple Grove was the actual scribe. It was his mind that bound together and put into words the strange experiences and knowledge of a coterie of ex-convicts,—men who had been in touch with violence and fraud and cunning. Not one of them could have written the Lestrange novels, but without their assistance, the novels themselves could not have taken form.

"Vivian Lestrange himself served seven years in gaol. His offence was embezzlement, but his sentence, like my own, was aggravated because he used violence in his endeavour to avoid what he always regarded as unfair arrest and imprisonment. Seven years was a savage sentence, but the man who tried him was known among our coterie as a savage judge. Vivian Lestrange has said to me that before his imprisonment he 'never performed any action that was unworthy of a gentleman,'—so ran his old-fashioned phrasing. Truly, prison doth make villains of us all! No man can live for seven years among criminals and remain himself unaltered. Prison is a levelling process,—a levelling down to the worst, not up to the best. I was once a fairly harmless lad—before my first conviction. Now I own no ethical code save my own comfort, my own profit, my own safety.

"Oh, you of His Majesty's Police—I know this letter will be read by one of you, oh immaculate men in dark blue—are you impatient with this long preamble? Read on, if for naught save duty's sake.

"I have dwelt on my own moral development in prison, because it was I who was the humble factor in the germination of one of the finest novelists of the day. We do not have much opportunity for philosophic discussions 'inside,' normal conversation with our fellows is forbidden to us, but will you deny, oh truthful reader in dark blue, that the old lag outwits your inhuman regulations? Have you heard of the prisoner's code in Princetown, rapped out on the iron hot-water pipes, so that convict communicates with convict, as day does to day in the 19th Psalm? Can you read Morse and the tick-tack code of the race-course, the thieves' jargon of Shadwell, and the patient tapping of the alphabet by illiterate men with time to spare? We talked, we enemies of society, in spite of all regulations; we even exchanged anecdotes at times. One day Vivian Lestrange said to me, 'What a novel one could write about all this!'

"Ah! but could one?... I have tried, but I had not the imagination to weld the strange fragments into a whole, to dress the fantastic story in human garb, to make it come alive. But Vivian Lestrange had that power. Later, when we were both free, we set about our strange collaboration. I knew many criminals, and one led to another, once they had learned that I would pay for a strange story. Have you read *The Charterhouse Case*, oh man in dark blue? Did you wonder how those details were amassed by a painstaking novelist? Ask at Princetown about old William Griggs,—he served ten years for assault with violence, and he died last year. It was he who told me those details of the moor. To save you much wearisome research, I will assure you now, that neither Lestrange nor I ever served in Princetown.

"Thus then the syndicate came into being, and 'Vivian Lestrange' took pen in hand and wove those strange true stories of his into a living whole, so cunningly that no one ever guessed the truth, yet with such artistry that the very lordliest of reviewers fell into the trick of superlatives before a Lestrange novel.

"It was a profitable business! Apart from other means of livelihood—believe me, we learnt more than the trades you taught us 'inside'—the Lestrange novels combined pleasure with profit to a variety of men and women whose portraits are ensconced in your Rogues' gallery at Scotland Yard. Why then did Lestrange leave the stage so suddenly?

"Men have short memories, and a little success may engender a lot of arrogance. He was so sure of his own security that he was going to tempt fate by describing one of the actual activities which enables me to live as a respected citizen of a prosperous provincial city today. I value my position; I am no uneducated upstart of the gutter. I went to a famous school once, and I lived as the prosperous middle classes like to live, in comfort and security. Here I have a position as a gentleman of independent means, with a background (quite fictitious) and a future (full of hope).

"I am known as a charitable man, and a churchgoer, I hope one day to be churchwarden,—that position, is, to my mind, the very zenith of middle class respectability.

"Yet I saw all this security in jeopardy, because the creative imagination of an obstinate author was bent on using my story as a theme in a Lestrange novel.

"One thing at least the law in this land has taught me,—that a man must be his own keeper, he must fend for himself.

"Lestrange was shot. He died without knowing that he was in danger, without fear, without suffering; his body is hidden away—and here is a situation which would have appealed to his ironical mind—in a spot which he himself described to me. When he was young, Lestrange was a country gentleman, and it is to his own county that he returned in death, to a spot whose potentialities as a hiding place he had discussed with me as he wove out the fabric of his last plot. 'It is the loneliest place in the world,' he told me, 'why not go there yourself one day and see it?—but take a pair of oars in your car lest old Dick has grown cautious with age. Don't go near the village for they are curious of strangers.'

"I have re-read what I have written, sitting in my car on a shady hill in the Cotswolds. It has quality, this narrative. I feel that if I sent it to the *Clarion*, for the first time in my life the *Clarion* would jump at a manuscript of mine,—but then I can devise no means of collecting payment—(I have not enough imagination, Lestrange could have helped me there).—Yet it is more satisfactory to think of a 'busy' spelling out my humble effort at authorship; I feel that there is a rich humour in the situation.

"One thing fails to satisfy me. What if the unimagi-native toilers of the police force dismiss this narrative as an imaginative effort on the part of some poor devil of an author? I must add chapter and verse to make my tale complete and convincing.

"Lestrange was shot (and you will find his body ere the autumn) with a service pistol,—a. 45. Here there was some bungling, I must admit. He was sitting in his chair at his study table, and he fell forward instantly when he was shot. I do not often suffer from nerves, but when I walked towards him across the room, I thought I saw a figure outside the window. I shot again,—quite needlessly. That involved me in some trouble, for I had meant to avoid all melodrama in this business. I knew that eventually the house would be searched by the police, (the lease soon comes to an end) and there was a broken window,—a maddening detail, for though I am neat with my hands I have never learnt the simple craft of putting in a pane of glass. I will not weary you with a recapitulation of my original plans. That broken pane of glass rendered them null and void. I acted quickly, and I admit that I spent an unwontedly busy evening in putting things to rights. (My convict's training made me a good house cleaner.)

"And the housekeeper, you will ask? I need only say precisely this. I have over her the same hold she might have over me. A life for a life,—and life for both of us is sweet. 'Mrs. Fife' will never give me away.

"In conclusion,—I apologise if I stress the obvious— may I suggest that you compare this typing with that on a packet recently sent to Miss Clarke? Lestrange had great faith in her judgment, and I am convinced that a young woman of such common sense would inform the police of the strange present which she has recently received. Those notes were drawn from the Bank as a payment to the Lestrange Syndicate, and Miss Clarke has by her competence deserved well of us. Needless to say, she had no knowledge of Lestrange's death. I alone am in possession of the facts, and quite frankly, I defy you to find me. For what it is worth I offer my advice. Save your faces. Say that Lestrange has been found and the mystery is at an end. Amnesia is a fashionable complaint. There will be no more Lestrange novels. I deplore it, but I value my own peace first. For me the future is to be one of unassailed respectability.

"Believe me to be, oh admirable man in dark blue,

"A PRODUCT OF THE PENAL SYSTEM."

Having read the typescript through three times, Bond sat back and sighed heavily.

"I'll be damned!" he hazarded, and "Well, I am, absolutely..." but he checked his soliloquy because he disliked swearing, and took up the telephone to get into touch with Chief Inspector Warner.

It was some hours later that the two men met,—in Warner's room at Scotland Yard,—because the Chief Inspector had been busy on his own devices that day.

"Hullo? What's she been up to now?" demanded Warner cheerfully, and Bond tossed the typescript down on the table.

"You're interested in literary style, sir," he said. "Perhaps you can tell me if this was composed by a man or by a woman."

Warner took up the envelope and applied himself to the contents. He read it through deliberately, without letting a muscle of his face move because he knew that Bond was watching him eagerly, but as he reached the end he said softly, "My holy aunt! I am absolutely—"

"So was I," put in Bond. "It just about took my breath away, I can tell you."

"Where are we now?" demanded Warner. "You want me to agree with you that this was written by Eleanor Clarke? Hang it all, Bond! I don't believe it."

"Neither do I," replied Bond, "but it's going to take a bit of explaining. Some of it's too true. Somebody knows everything. There's very little to be gleaned from the detective's point of view, though. I verified the reference William Griggs, and that's perfectly true. He died at Deptford last year."

"Did he, by Jove!" said Warner, with a sudden interest in his tone, and then continued, "look here, let's go through this closely and précis the contents. First, Vivian Lestrange compiled his novels from actual happenings confided to him by ex-convicts. Well, it's possible. Granted that a man was naturally a first-rate novelist, he could take the germ of an idea and elaborate it. I wouldn't say it was impossible. The author of this letter claims to have been a go-between. I wonder if he—or she—visited Lestrange or vice versa…"

"No evidence, sir," said Bond gruffly. "There was often a heavy post at Temple Grove. Maybe the whole thing was done by correspondence."

"The modern method," said Warner. "Let us teach you by post. Earn while learning. See the advertisements… Next, Vivian Lestrange served seven years—like Jacob—and so did Edward Merstham. That is point one. We must look up the judge, by the way. Sounds a bit like old Blackcap. He loved to 'larn' them…

My own moral development… H'm… that's all poppycock. It's quite true about the tapping conversations in Princetown, but every Tom, Dick and Harry knows that… 'To weld the strange fragments into a whole, to dress the fantastic story in human garb.' There's a style about it, you know. Well balanced phrases and all that. I see the practised hand here."

"Too many adjectives about it for my liking," said Bond. "They simply stick out. The whole thing is too flowery."

"Meaning too feminine—oh immaculate man in dark blue? Good Lord, if this weren't so serious, it'd be damned funny. In fact it is damned funny… William Griggs,—fact corroborated. That's point two. Meanwhile Vivian Lestrange got over confident and 'tempted fate.' That's a cliché. He could have done better than that… All this about public schools and churchwardens is just eye-wash. I don't believe it. Lestrange was shot… so was our chappy in the chimney space… he was a country gentleman. That's point three. You've got to admit that our stylish correspondent seemed to know the Merstham story. 'Take a pair of oars in your car, etc.' That sounds like Kirkham-on-Wye,—we'll make that point four. The next item is the broken window, which proves that the writer knew Temple Grove and also the name of the housekeeper. Finally the comment on Miss Clarke's little present and the unsolicited testimonial… You know, that girl never wrote this, Bond. She's too much common sense. It looks as though she's protesting her own innocence vicariously and she would have seen the unwisdom of it, to say nothing of the lack of artistry."

"I think she would have been quick enough to see your reactions to that paragraph," said Bond with one of his sudden flashes of shrewdness. "She always sees the sentence after next.

That's what I don't like about her. She's too ready to force consequences."

"As you are to detect corollaries," laughed Warner. "Let's sum up our facts and omit debatable factors. Here are my points:

"1. Vivian Lestrange served a sentence of seven years (as did Edward Merstham).
2. Existence of William Griggs.
3. Vivian Lestrange was once a country gentleman—(as was Edward Merstham).
4. Knowledge of Kirkham and Dick Barton's boat.
5. Broken window at Temple Grove.
6. Name of Mrs. Fife.
7. Knowledge of Eleanor Clarke's parcel.

I suppose I can add as point 8 that the typescript of Miss Clarke's anonymous gift and the typescript of this letter are identical?"

"You can, sir," agreed Bond.

"Now how much of this knowledge could have been amassed by Eleanor Clarke?" said Warner.

"*Point* 1. If Vivian Lestrange served seven years' penal servitude, I doubt very much if he would have confided that fact to his secretary, and judging from what we have seen of the inside of Temple Grove, he wasn't the type of man to leave evidence about for other people to speculate upon.

"*Point* 2. Next the evidence of Griggs. Unless she had acquaintances herself in the criminal world, Eleanor Clarke couldn't have known of Griggs' existence.

"*Points* 3 *and* 4, concerning Kirkham, come under the same heading as Point 1.

"It is improbable that she ever heard of the place from Lestrange. The last three points would have been known to her all right, provided she was cognisant of the murder."

"Looking at it in another way, sir, you could make out a case along these lines," said Bond. "If Miss Clarke is either principal or an accessory in the shooting of that man whom you found at Kirkham, one can assume that she knew all about him,—both his history and origin. It's not to be assumed that she shot him just casually."

"No," agreed Warner. "I grant you that she's not a casual character. You've altered your line of thought, these last days, Bond," went on the Chief Inspector pleasantly. "At first you refused to admit that Vivian Lestrange existed except in the person of his secretary."

Bond flushed. "Yes, sir. I have been floundering from the beginning, trying to get a definite bearing, and then losing myself again. I realise you've got the laugh of me, but I can still make out a case, though it's not a very shipshape one. I started as you say, with the possibility in my mind that Miss Clarke herself was Lestrange, and that the whole story she told was a put up yarn to serve her own ends. The main difference in the outlook now is that we have found a corpse, and we know that it's a case of murder we're investigating. I still maintain that there is no proof that the corpse ever lived in Temple Grove, and that there is quite a possibility that Miss Clarke could have posted herself that packet of notes, and could have written this letter here."

"And Mrs. Fife?"

"She is either an accessory or principal. One woman alone couldn't have moved that body, but two could have managed it all right."

Bond studied Warner's face ruefully, but the Chief Inspector merely said:

"Go on. You've got some more ideas to come," and Bond plunged on.

"We don't know where the dead man was killed. Assume for argument's sake that the shooting was at Temple Grove, on Saturday, or even on Friday. His body could have been driven to Kirkham on Saturday itself. We've no corroborative evidence that Miss Clarke was in London on Saturday. We only know that she was observed on Sunday about eleven a.m. That would have given her time to get to Kirkham by Saturday evening, help move the corpse after dark and then get home again by Sunday morning and slip in unobserved."

Warner shook his head. "It won't quite do. The cottage wasn't burned until after the Sunday—probably not until after Eleanor Clarke came to see you... Not that I'm denying that your argument might hold water in a slightly altered guise. The devil of it is that this confounded letter leaves us all at sea. It's difficult to believe that there's any truth in it, only we're brought smack up against it by the fact that the writer knows certain points which no one unconnected with the case *could* know. I think the best thing I can do is to tell you the line I've been following myself, and then we'll see if we can read some sense into the whole riddle."

CHAPTER XI

"THE LINE" WHICH WARNER HAD BEEN FOLLOWING WAS in the direction of Michael Ashe. Since his "hunch" about the taxi driver had proved correct (so the Chief Inspector argued) it seemed definitely worth while to make an effort at interviewing Ashe, if only to see if he could be induced to part with information concerning Lestrange. Since the publishers could give him no information as to the novelist's whereabouts, Warner went to his club,—the Addison, in John Street. This club he discovered had been founded by a coterie of essayists shortly before the war, but it had entirely altered its character of recent years. The members of the Addison (it was only a small club) were now recruited among writers of travel books, explorers, wanderers, geographers and—as Warner guessed—a certain number of adventurers, whose originality and versatility commended themselves to the club committee. It was not enough to be a writer if you wished to join the Addison, you must also have been a traveller, a war correspondent, a secret service man or a sailor.

When Warner approached the club secretary, a man named Mason,—with a request for information concerning the whereabouts of Michael Ashe, he was met with a laugh.

"Ashe? I'm afraid I can't tell you. He's one of those chaps who plays a lone hand. I saw him last about ten days ago, when he gave up his room,—he'd been staying here for a few days. I believe he was going to Majorca, but I can't be certain."

"Will a letter be forwarded?" enquired Warner, and the other shrugged his shoulders.

"It'll be forwarded to his bank," he replied. Seeing that he was not going to get any further on these lines Warner produced his official card, and Mason stared at it with raised eyebrows. "Very interesting," he said, "but as I have told you all that I know, I'm afraid I can't do any more."

Warner settled himself more firmly in his chair, and smiled pleasantly at the other.

"I want to get hold of Ashe, because I think he can give me some important information," he rejoined.

"Quite," said the other blandly. "Quite."

"I've no doubt you'll be able to help me more than you realise," went on Warner. "For instance you can tell me if Ashe used this club as his *pied-à-terre*. After all, everybody—no matter how much they travel,—has got to have some place where they keep their permanent possessions. Even the least acquisitive are liable to have belongings which they don't want to trail round the world with them."

Seeing the expression on the other man's face, Warner added, "I mean of course inanimate belongings,—trunks, books, and so on."

Mason allowed himself a chuckle. "Quite. You want to know if Ashe used this place as a depository. He certainly did not. When he stayed here he only brought a couple of grips, and took them away again when he left. As to whether he kept up any sort of permanent establishment, I can't tell you. Ashe isn't forthcoming, you know."

"So I have been told," said Warner. "Who put him up for membership here?"

"Old Gresson,—Philip Gresson, you know, the man who writes all that stuff about the Peruvian civilisations. I believe he met Ashe in South America, sitting under a juniper tree in the wilderness, or something like that."

"How long has Ashe been a member?"

"Two years. Most of the time he's been abroad, but he's been in London, on and off, for the last six months."

"Is Mr. Gresson in London?"

"Lord, no! He went back to Peru eighteen months ago, and no one has heard of him since. We've almost given him up."

Leaning back in his chair Mason studied Warner thoughtfully. "Not being very helpful, am I? Quite honestly, if my life depended on it, I couldn't give you any information about Ashe. He's as close as an oyster."

"Do you like him?" asked Warner, suddenly, and the other gave him a short laugh.

"No, I don't. He's as conceited as Lucifer and as obstinate as a mule, and he'll argue black's white without any evidence but his own blasted opinion... How's the Lestrange case going?"

"So so," replied Warner in his placid way. "Why?"

Mason shrugged his shoulders. "Scotland Yard is busy looking for one celebrated author, about whose origin and private life nobody knows anything; then Scotland Yard comes and calls here and asks questions about Michael Ashe,—another well-known writer about whose origin and private life nobody knows anything... I can't tell you where Ashe is now, but I can tell you that he's been trying to find out who Vivian Lestrange is. It's my business to know a bit about writers in general, and Ashe tried to pump me about Lestrange."

"What do you know about Lestrange?" enquired Warner.

"Nothing. Nobody knows him,—but I was a bit tired of Ashe and his God almighty manner, and I just dropped a hint in his hearing that I knew Lestrange. Ashe promptly asked me to dine with him at the Savoy, and did his best to make me drunk... You'd hardly credit it, but I could drink Ashe blind and still be sober myself, so he wasted his money. It annoyed him, so he tried to make trouble between me and the committee here."

"Well that's extremely interesting," said Warner. "It's obviously of no use for me to ask you to dine in the hope that you'll tell me all about Vivian Lestrange, or even Michael Ashe..."

"No. I'm afraid it's not," said Mason. "Look here. I've got my job to consider, and I've already said a spot more than discretion permits. When I told you that I didn't know anything about Michael Ashe, I was telling you the exact truth, but other people might know a bit more. Will you guarantee to me that this conversation is confidential? I don't want to be put into the witness-box and cross-examined as to what I've said about members of the Addison."

"You're not likely to be," replied Warner. "I can promise you that anything you tell me, which will enable me to get into touch with Ashe, will not be repeated. I'll see that you're not brought into it."

"Good. The only thing I can tell you is this. Ashe was yarning here one day with a fellow named Staunton. The latter is a retired Admiral who was in the China Squadron for years. From what I overheard of the conversation, Staunton thought he'd seen Ashe before,—some question of a Court of Enquiry, I believe—and Ashe was a bit over emphatic in telling Staunton he was mistaken."

"Where's Staunton to be found? In Peru?"

Mason laughed. "No. He comes into lunch here at one o'clock every day as regular as clockwork. You can catch him all right. The point is that you mustn't tell him that I repeated what I'd overheard of a private conversation between members. He's a punctilious old bird."

Warner nodded. "I see. I expect I can find a way of avoiding that difficulty. Since Admiral Staunton is a member here, I take it he is a writer?"

"Quite correct. He's written some volumes of reminiscences, one about the Boxer Rebellion in 1900,—Staunton was a snotty on Beatty's ship, the *Barfleur*,—and several books dealing with cruises in the Malay Archipelago. *A Sailor in the Philippines* and *From Bangkok to Singapore* are his best known."

"Very useful of him," said Warner, "because Ashe has written about the same part of the world—you remember *Allen of the Andamans*?"

"Yes, like his damned cheek," said Mason. "Ashe thinks he's a second Conrad, and actually challenges the comparison by writing about the Malays. He's not fit to weed Conrad's grave."

"Maybe," said Warner, "but Ashe is a damned fine writer and comparisons are 'oderous.' Now have you got any of Staunton's books anywhere in this place?"

"Yes. In the library. He always gives us a presentation copy. More than Ashe does."

"Well, take me up to the library, there's a good chap," said Warner, "and when Staunton comes in, tell him I want to see him."

"Chief Inspector, or plain Mister?" demanded Mason.

"Chief Inspector. Give him my card—or tell the porter to do so," replied Warner, "and many thanks for all your help."

"Not at all. Do you really think Ashe knows anything about Lestrange?"

"The Lord knows," replied Warner. "Since you've told me that Ashe was interested in Lestrange, my desire to meet him is doubled. Nice place you've got here. Those Adam chaps were damn fine architects."

Mason, leading the way to the library of the club, took Warner's cue and talked intelligently of mouldings and ceilings, panelling and proportion as they went up the fine wide staircase.

It was nearly half an hour later that a page-boy told Warner that Admiral Staunton was in the smoking-room, and the Chief Inspector led thither found himself face to face with a square-shouldered, grey-haired man, whose aspect managed to combine an effect of energy, aggressiveness, intense propriety, and childlike simplicity. Warner, glancing round, was relieved to see that the room in which they stood was a small annexe to the smoking-room proper, and that there was no one present but themselves. Staunton held Warner's card in his hand, and looked at its owner with some suspicion.

"I like to know where I stand, sir," he barked. "Is this an official visit?"

"Inasmuch as I am on duty, it is, sir," replied Warner. "I admit that some apology is called for, because it is quite probable that I am troubling you needlessly, but I am here in the hope that you can give my department assistance in the way of information."

This carefully considered speech was favourably received.

"Very glad to help you if it is in my power. Regard the police very favourably, very favourably indeed. Very competent body of men, very civil and obliging. What's it all about? Sit down, Chief Inspector, sit down."

"It is an entirely confidential matter, sir. I have been trying to get into touch with a man who seems to be in the habit of going away and leaving no address. Now it happens that this man has written a good deal about the Malay Archipelago, the Gulf of Siam and the China Sea. I knew of you as an authority concerning these parts, and when I discovered that you and the man I am trying to communicate with were members of the same club, I took it on myself to ask you for this interview."

"Hump! You're after Michael Ashe?"

The abruptness of the retort made Warner smile inwardly.

"Not in the usual sense, sir. I only want to get into touch with him to ask him for information."

"Hump! Well, you started by saying this conversation was to be regarded as confidential. I take it that's binding on both parties. I've no desire to be had up for slander."

"You need not concern yourself there, sir," replied Warner. "What you say to me will go no farther."

"Glad to hear it. What I say is that Ashe may be a damned scoundrel. I can't give you chapter and verse, but I suspect it. When a man's got nothing better than suspicion to go on, he should have the *nous* to keep quiet,—but when it comes to a police enquiry, damn it, he's justified in saying what he thinks—always understood that it's surmise, and not facts he's stating."

"Yes. I see that point, sir," agreed Warner. "If you can give me any information at all about Ashe, I shall be very glad to hear it. I'm in a bit of a quandary, because I may have got a bee in my bonnet over him, and I'm quite prepared to discover he's not the man I want at all."

"Hump! What do you know about him?"

"Nothing at all, except that during the last two years he has been well to the fore as a writer, and it appears that he knows his subject."

"Yes, you're right there. Ashe knows what he is writing about, and nobody's better qualified to criticise him than I am. Well, here's my story. In 1924, I was retired, axed, to put it shortly, and I was returning to England from Hong Kong after twenty-five years' service in the China Squadron. If you've read Ashe's books—and mine,—you know what a typhoon means. Between Hong Kong and Singapore we went considerably out of our course to avoid the path of a hurricane which swept across the eastern side of the China Sea. I won't bother you with our exact bearings, but to put it in plain language we were mid-way between the coast of Annam and the Philippine Islands—latitude about 15' north, longitude 115' east, to give you a rough idea. Weather had cleared, barometer rising, wind very slight, and a smooth sea. At mid-day we sighted a small vessel to starboard. Now we were best part of a hundred miles off the ordinary trade route, and the sight of a small open boat in these waters only meant one thing. We altered our course and hove to, and then lowered a boat to investigate. There were five men in the boat we'd sighted, and the only one who appeared to be alive was a big fellow sitting by the tiller—holding on to it, though he was a long way past steering. He was a white man, and there was another lying across the thwarts. The others were Lascars, of whom one was still alive, but went raving mad when he recovered consciousness. Well, when the white fellow became capable of answering questions, this was his story. He'd been one of the crew of the *S.S. Flores*, bound from Manila to Singapore with a cargo of hemp. The *Flores* had run into the typhoon and made heavy weather of it, then when they thought they'd got through the worst of it, their propeller shaft snapped. That convey anything to you?"

Warner grinned. "I can use my imagination, sir. Isn't it a fact that in a typhoon, the correct procedure is to run with the wind?"

"Run with the wind on the starboard quarter," barked Staunton. "In this case the wind had veered and the storm had begun to move eastward. They couldn't heave to, and they'd had a heavy bucketing. The vessel, being disabled, shipped seas all over her, and eventually the master gave orders to lower the boats. How that boat we picked up ever lived in such a sea it's not for me to say,—but there she was, with the first mate, one white sailorman, and half a dozen Lascars. When they had a chance to think about it, they discovered that their water casks weren't filled. To cut a long story short, they'd been four days without water. The mate had had a crack on the head when the boat was lowered, and the sun had done the rest. Two of the Lascars tried drinking sea water and went crazy. Jumped overboard,—so he said. Maybe. The white sailor had joined the *Flores* at Manila; his name was Thomas Brown."

"Good Lord!" exclaimed Warner, and then he apologised for his interruption.

"You can take it from me it was a funny story. In fact, a damned funny story," growled Staunton. "It wasn't my business,—I wasn't holding a court of enquiry; that came later at Singapore where we landed Brown, but I wasn't satisfied with any of it. That chap Brown was too stupid: he didn't know anything about anything. The ship's course wasn't his business. He was only working his way back to Singapore, and when they'd taken to the boats, he helped the mate get their boat clear of the *Flores*. They didn't want to be broken up crashing against the ship's side. When they abandoned her, the *Flores* was sinking by the stern; two other boats had been launched and the Captain was in the last of them, but they lost sight of one another in the storm.

"Well, I suppose the court of enquiry had to make the best of it. None of the other boats were picked up and Brown was the only witness they'd got. It's no use expecting a seaman to tell you why the Captain did this or that or the other, or exactly the position of the vessel at a given time. No. But I give you my word, sir, there was dirty work somewhere."

Suddenly he studied Warner's face and then gave a little chuckle.

"And what's all this to do with you? A vessel called the *Flores*, registered under the Siamese flag, is disabled by a typhoon in the China Sea and goes to the bottom, a total loss, and only one man is left alive to tell what happened to her. I'm babbling, eh? Maybe. That man who survived did well for himself. He goes by the name of Michael Ashe nowadays."

"Well, I'm damned!" said Warner, and the other nodded sympathetically.

"You may well be. How do you think I knew him again? The man I knew was bearded, worn to the bone and scorched like a brick; dressed in oddments our crew had given him after he was picked up. I went to talk to him,—not officially, mind you, I was a passenger on that trip—but because I was interested. One of the things I noticed was that he'd the hell of a long scar right up his left forearm, from wrist to elbow. It happened that Ashe was yarning in here one day, talking about wrestling, and he and another fellow took off their coats to demonstrate some trick or other. Ashe tore his shirt-sleeve while they were wrestling and it was stripped off his arm. When I saw that scar again, I knew why something about him had seemed familiar to me,—though I hadn't been able to place him. Then I knew. I'd last seen him on the *Oranga*. He was Thomas Brown."

"Did you ask him about it?"

"Ask him? I should say I did! And he denied it. Gave me the lie. I tell you I can't prove it,—but it's true."

Leaning forward, Staunton pointed at Warner with a finger which seemed to accuse him.

"That man Brown played a part as an uneducated, uncouth seaman, with a vocabulary of a couple of hundred words, and a mind like a monkey's—a slow, stupid, half baked son of a drunken sea cook, a blasted imbecile who wasn't fit to shovel coal in a bunker, the sort of seaman who wasn't anything but human cargo,—and eight years later I came across him as a member of a literary club. Damn it! the man's a scoundrel,—follows, doesn't it?"

"As to that, you're a better judge than I am, sir," said Warner. "I suppose when the enquiry was held, they'd have found out who signed on at Manila,—the ship's company would have been known?"

"Yes, yes. That was clear enough. Thomas Brown had had his discharge from a vessel trading between Surabaya and Manila; he'd joined the *Flores* at the last moment because one of their hands had gone sick. My own idea is that the owners of the *Flores* wanted her scuppered. She was heavily insured and the underwriters had to pay up. There's been dirty work of that sort before and will be again, but the interesting part of this story is the re-emergence of Thomas Brown in Michael Ashe."

Warner sat down in a brown study, doing a mental jig-saw puzzle, and feeling that every time he tried adding a piece to his framework, he had to scrap all the previously arranged pieces.

Staunton, puffing away at a very foul pipe, said at length,

"That wasn't the sort of story you expected to hear?" and Warner came back to the present with a jerk.

"Well, no, sir. Not exactly. I'm very much obliged to you for telling me about it, because in my job we're always amassing little bits of evidence and trying to fit them together. What I want now is to make contact with Ashe, but from what you've told me, it may be the devil of a business. He's one of these men with a capacity for a dual life. If he wants to slip away, he can just turn seaman again. The only thing about that is that there are so many seamen unemployed that he wouldn't stand a good chance of getting a job. Still, if he has plenty of friends at various ports, he could probably work a bit of graft. How long ago was it that you challenged him as Thomas Brown?"

"Three weeks,—I've hardly seen the fellow since. He tried to laugh it off,—but he didn't like it,—I know that."

"How did you put it to him?" asked Warner.

"Why, simply enough. I said 'Good God! Weren't you once picked up by the *Oranga* after your vessel was wrecked in the China Sea?' He looked at me like the devil himself."

"Thought you were the devil himself, more likely, sir," chuckled Warner.

"Hump!... You've probably heard that he was talking about going to Majorca? Yes? Well, that's the last place you'll find him, in my opinion. Honolulu or the Andaman Islands are more likely."

"He's bound to turn up some time, sir," said Warner. "Having established himself as Michael Ashe, he won't want to cast off that very profitable personality without a good reason."

"Maybe he has a good reason," growled Staunton. "I believe I rattled him up a bit. Let me know when you come across him."

"I will," said Warner cheerfully,—and he did.

CHAPTER XII

ONCE MORE WARNER AND BOND SAT IN CONSULTATION over the "Missing Author Case,"—thus had the Press labelled the mystery of Vivian Lestrange,—"to report progress," or lack of it, as Bond suggested in his sceptical way. "Co-ordination is the business on the agenda," said Warner cheerfully. "It's a lovely word, suggesting a sort of orderly creativeness,—emergent evolution, y'know. We want to connect up 'the recluse of Temple Grove' (as our informative letter writer put it) with the chap in the chimney at Kirkham. Incidentally, they managed to keep that inquest pretty quiet, and adjourned 'pending further investigations' before the local Press had a chance to realise the possibilities of the occasion. Now the more I think of it, the more am I disposed to be hopeful about Vargon's suggestion that the Merstham brothers are our real quarry, and as an alternative title to the Merstham brothers I'm disposed to read Vivian Lestrange and Michael Ashe. You read the report of the prison people concerning Edward Merstham. The salient points are as follows:—Born in 1884. Height 5 feet 11 inches. Excellent teeth. Very long hands and feet. Cephalic Index 74.5. Weight in 1924, 12 stone 10 lb. When I showed a copy of Edward Merstham's photograph, taken in prison, to Miss Clarke, she promptly said she didn't recognise it, but there's nothing in that. Merstham was clean shaven and close-cropped. Lestrange bearded and shaggy and ten years older. Of course she didn't recognise that wooden, expressionless face of the prison photograph. Details of colouring, finger-prints and so on, don't help us so far, but the dimensions of that corpse are the same as those of either James or Edward Merstham,—they were very much of a size. Now, in addition to the official report from the prison authorities, concerning Edward Merstham, I've got this letter from the padre who was chaplain at Maidstone when Merstham was imprisoned there. Read it yourself."

Bond took the letter from Warner and studied it.

"I remember Merstham very well," wrote the chaplain, "and I had a good many talks with him. During the first months of his sentence he was taciturn to a degree, and resented any efforts to get into touch with him. Later, as he became more accustomed to his environment, he became more approachable, but he was always very bitter. He harped persistently on the fact that he was unjustly sentenced, but later on, his mind took a more philosophic turn, and he used to discuss the ethics of punishment, maintaining that he, who was being unfairly punished, would be justified in meting out retribution to the author of his own misfortunes. He always came back to this theme in any of our talks. For instance, he took an exaggerated interest in the book of Job, and his biblical researches were a matter of embarrassment to me because he was always asking me for my opinion on such drastic punishments as those meted out to Ananias and Sapphira, Lot's wife, the informers against Daniel, and so forth."

Bond broke out into a chuckle. "I reckon this chaplain had a tough job expounding the theme of 'Vengeance is mine' to a man on whom the vengeance of the State had fallen pretty heavily," he observed.

"Apart from this obsession," continued the letter, "I should say that one of the few benefits imprisonment conferred on him was that it induced him to read seriously for the first time in his life. He read a lot of solid stuff,—Gibbon and Macaulay, then the works of Addison, Steele and Swift. Later he took to more modern essayists, and his judgment became very acute. He was a good workman too, and became an expert bookbinder, as well as mastering the complexities of type-setting. He would have earned the maximum remission of his sentence, but he was involved in assisting another prisoner's escape. After this incident he became troublesome because he persistently broke the rules about not communicating with his fellow convicts whenever he could make an opportunity of doing so.

"He had no visitors, and neither wrote nor received letters. At the conclusion of his sentence, when I had a few words with him to wish him well, and to offer him any assistance that was in my power, he said that he felt he was leaving that prison at least with a fixed purpose,—and I fear that the purpose in his mind was far from being a desirable one.

"In conclusion I should say that he was a man of more than usual mental ability, but embittered and impossible to influence."

"H'm. Very interesting, but hardly informative, sir," said Bond.

"This is where we use our imagination and apportion parts to our case," replied Warner.

"That description seems to me as though it might very well be applied to Vivian Lestrange,—in which case we can envisage him (alias Edward Merstham) sitting carefully concealed at Temple Grove, hoping for a chance to have a go at brother James one day, while James roams the world, keeping a weather-eye open for any sign of brother Edward."

"Accepting that hypothesis, I suppose that brother James felt that he could never be absolutely secure while Edward was still alive to testify against him," ruminated Bond.

"That makes sense, because fear often begets violence. In which case you assume that James—alias Michael Ashe wrote the 'Penal Product' letter out of sheer joie de vivre, so to speak."

Warner chuckled a little. "I bet he enjoyed the writing of it," he observed, and Bond went on "You've got a very pretty line of reasoning to account for your facts, sir, though the whole argument depends on catching Michael Ashe and getting him identified as James Merstham. Meanwhile, what about the housekeeper?"

"Once again, nothing but assumptions," replied Warner, "the old 'either-or' again. Mrs. Fife either assisted the murderer, or else she was disposed of at the same time as Lestrange. I favour the first suggestion, because two corpses would have been rather a handful for one murderer. If you invert the parts and arrange for one corpse and two murderers the thing is considerably simplified."

It was Bond's turn to chuckle. "A further variation suggests a couple each way," he said. "You've got the necessary actors,—Lestrange and Mrs. Fife,—Miss Clarke and Michael Ashe."

"Meanwhile, to find Michael Ashe is point one on the agenda," said Warner. "I can't find any traces of a permanent habitation for him, but he certainly possessed a car. I'm advertising for it. It's a 1934 Vauxhall Cadet, Saloon body, sunshine roof, Dunlop tyres. Registration number A.B. 7469X."

"By jove!" exclaimed Bond. "This sounds as though we might be able to rely a little more on facts and a little less on guessing. I've been worrying the Temple Grove neighbourhood silly about cars, and not learnt a thing for my trouble until this morning, when the Mallings' came back from abroad—you remember that they are the next door neighbours to Temple Grove. I had had a look round their premises to see that everything was ship-shape; there's a garage, but there was no car in it. I assumed that the Mallings' took their car abroad with them. Silly to assume anything of course. Today I learnt that they don't possess a car, but nevertheless a car had been standing recently in their garage, *and* it had Dunlop tyres, practically unused."

"This is an intriguing story," mused Warner. "At first it seemed so involved, and now it's beginning to resolve itself into a beautiful simplicity. Ashe having found Lestrange, must have realised that the very secretiveness of the latter's mode of living simplified the murderer's job for him. I know it looks like jumping to conclusions, but I do think one point bears out our present theory and that is the fact that Michael Ashe and Vivian Lestrange have both been invisible since that same week-end. The last I can hear of Ashe is that he left the Addison on that Saturday in his own car, a couple of suitcases in the back of it, with the avowed intention of taking the car abroad with him.

So far as we can tell at present, he didn't follow out that part of his plan, for the cross-channel authorities have no record of trans-shipping the Vauxhall."

"Yet the whole thing is the most exasperating network of assumptions, sir," said Bond. "We've no proof that any of our surmises are right. If you want a list of hard facts, cutting out theories of any kind, this is what we've got:

(1) An unidentified corpse with a bullet in its brain and the remains of the Lestrange pocket-book ready to hand.
(2) A packet of Treasury notes, paid out to Lestrange's cheque, received through the post by Miss Clarke.
(3) A letter from someone with an imagination who knew the calibre of the bullet in the brain of the corpse.

"Damn it all. It's like the house that Jack built."

"While your mind harps continually on hard facts, mine goes a-whoring after its own inventions, as the psalmist has it," replied Warner. "I can't help thinking that this fellow Ashe is tied up in the business somehow. He's so damned à-propos, with his nosing round after Lestrange, and while I grant you that Dunlop tyres are about as common as blackberries, I still cherish a secret conviction that Master Ashe paid Lestrange a visit that Saturday and paid up some back reckoning. The odd thing is that both Lestrange and Ashe seem to lack a background. I've been on to the Foreign Office, thinking I could get a photograph of Ashe from his passport duplicates, but he hasn't had a passport issued to him in this country. There's nothing much in that, of course, because he may have got one in one of the Dominions, or from a Consul in a foreign country. Any scamp can get a passport if he wants one, it's simply a matter of getting someone to sign an application. Trying the Merstham theory again, one can assume that if James Merstham became metamorphosed into Michael Ashe, he probably left this country on a cattle boat, or some craft of that kind, and eventually got taken on as a seaman bobbing up in mid-career in the China Sea, if Staunton's to be trusted. Funny he should have called himself Thomas Brown,—that's another link, you know. Perhaps both the Merstham's had an affection for *Tom Brown's School Days*... unless Edward fell under the spell of *Religio Medici* while he was in quod."

Rather to Bond's relief,—for the Chief Inspector's flights of fancy were not entirely to his liking—the telephone bell cut Warner's speech short, and Bond soon learned what the message was about.

"Ashe's car—in a garage at Southampton"—Warner threw the quick sentence in an aside to Bond, during the course of a longish conversation over the 'phone. Having hung up the receiver, Warner said: "The Vauxhall was left in a garage close by the docks on Monday morning, 16th April, by Ashe himself, according to the bloke in the garage. It's me for Southampton. I want to get in touch with Ashe; it seems to me he's our one concrete hope. Do you realise that apart from him, we haven't a notion in the wide world as to who may be at the bottom of this story?"

Bond made a sound like a snort, which might have been indicative of mirth or disgust, or a blending of both.

"I don't mind dealing with proper criminals, but heaven defend me from any more novelists, sir," he groaned; "there's nothing too lurid for the mind of one of those thriller merchants. Perhaps they got tired of merely writing about corpses, and took to body snatching. Planted that one on us at Kirkham for the pleasure of watching police methods at close quarters... You'll find Michael Ashe will have an alibi in Timbuctoo for the week-end which interests us, and probably next day a new Lestrange novel will be published in America, *Policemen at Play*. 'All characters in this work are purely fictitious.' If you have no further need for me at the present moment, sir, I'll get back to my own beat. I've a nice little case on hand about thefts from letter-boxes."

"You're a queer chap, Bond," said Warner. "You've got an imagination, but you won't trust it."

"No, by gum, I won't, sir," said Bond. "There's too much imagination flying around in this case. I've been investigating the life of a man whom no one's seen but his secretary, and I've been investigating the life of a secretary whose past defies inspection because the only people who could answer questions about her are dead, and whose present acquaintances can't tell you enough to make a half page report. The one and only fact I've collected is that a car stood in the Mallings' garage while they were abroad, and that it had no business to stand there, and if this is a case of novelists being humorous, one of them probably put the car there for a spot of local colour."

"*Dum spiro spero*," said Warner. "Good luck to your letter-boxes."

Arrived at Southampton, Warner found Lecky's Garage conveniently situated for the docks and the boat trains. The proprietor, a rotund little man—greeted the Chief Inspector cheerfully and invited him into his "office," a grubby glory-hole with walls of match boarding partitioned off from the main space of the garage. Here he cleared a chair for Warner beside a desk, covered with an amazing litter of papers and oddments, on which Lecky balanced himself, and then said, "What's up? Was that car pinched?"

"Not to my knowledge," replied Warner. "The sole reason we advertised for it was that we wanted to get in touch with the owner in order to get some information from him. He seems to have gone abroad and we can't find him. Now say if you can tell me exactly what happened when that car was brought in."

"It was on Monday morning, the 16th, at 11.30 a.m.," said Lecky promptly. "A big chap, who was driving pulled up outside here and came in, evidently in the devil of a hurry. He'd got the off wing of his car buckled up, the running board splintered and a good deal of scratching done to the body-work. Told me he had fouled a gate post taking a corner and got delayed while he was driving hard to catch the boat. He said he was going abroad for a couple of weeks and wanted to leave the car here for repairs and overhaul, and he'd pick it up again on his return journey... That was all right," said Lecky with a wink. "It's a nice car, this season's model in fact; what you'd call good security. I shouldn't part with the car again till he'd paid up for the doings, see?"

"Yes, I see," replied Warner, with that pleasant smile of his, that helped him such a lot in examining witnesses. "Can you tell me what the chap was like?—give me as much detail as you can."

"Say six foot tall, or jolly near it," said Lecky. "Dressed in a good grey Burberry and nice Trilby hat. Good leather gauntlets and a striped silk scarf round his neck. He was clean shaven, fairish sort of hair I think, but going grey... light coloured eyes and shaggy eyebrows... Sun burnt, good teeth... That's about the best I can do. He was what you'd call a noticeable chap. Age, oh about fiftyish."

"That's much better than most people can do in the way of descriptions," said Warner encouragingly. "Did he have any luggage with him?"

"Just a suitcase,—he lugged it out himself and walked off with it. He gave me his card,—here you are—and said he'd be back within three weeks and he'd expect the car to be ready for him. I said that'd be all O.K., and off he went. It's not more than a couple o' hundred yards to the quay-side from here you know."

"How did he walk? Any sign of a limp?"

"No, I don't think so. Look here! You're not going to tell me that chap isn't the owner of the blooming 'bus, are you? I reckon I've got to be paid for the job, anyway. A new wing I got, the other was crumpled to blazes and all..."

"No need to worry as far as I know," replied Warner. "The description you've given me fits the real owner all right. Now let me have a look at the Vauxhall."

"Don't go spoiling my good paint work," begged Lecky. "She's over here. Oh, by the way, I took out all the oddments and locked 'em up. You never can tell in a place like this."

"What were the oddments?"

"Oh, rugs, an old coat, maps and an A.A. book. They're in that cupboard in the corner."

Following Lecky across the garage to the corner indicated, Warner had a look at the "oddments." The first thing he examined was a map of Herefordshire, showing Ross and its surroundings. There were other maps covering the whole of the south of England, as well as a continental timetable. The coat was an old Aquascutum, with Ashe's name inside the pocket and a very crumpled old bill which proved to be a receipt for a meal in a Paris restaurant two years ago. There were two big heavy rugs, both of them dark coloured and showing signs of wear. Warner then proceeded to examine the inside of the Vauxhall; since he didn't expect to find any evidence in it, he was not disappointed at drawing a blank. One thing was certain, the car was Ashe's car, it contained his belongings, and according to Lecky, it had been left at the garage on Monday morning, the 16th.

"Well, what about it?" demanded the garage proprietor.

"It seems a nice car and you're making a good job of it," said Warner. "I think I'll take these maps and the A.A. book with me. I'll give you a receipt for them. If Mr. Ashe turns up unexpectedly for them, you can say the maps have got mislaid. No one with any sense leaves things loose in a car,—and when he turns up you can get on to the phone to the police station here just as fast as you like, and let them know he's on the premises. You needn't fill her up ready for him you know."

"Then there's another point," went on Warner, leading the way back to the small office. "I've told you that I want to see Mr. Ashe to ask him for information; don't go getting wild ideas into your head because I've taken charge of his maps, and don't go talking to anyone else about the subject. If Mr. Ashe comes back here and finds you've been spreading stories about him being wanted by the police, it'll be bad for your business to say nothing of risks of the defamation of character variety."

"All right. I'm not such a mug as I look," replied Lecky cheerfully. "I don't want to get wrong with the police, and I don't want a sock on the jaw from Mr. Ashe, but you might tell me,—speaking as one chap to another,—if you really think he will come back and claim his car?"

"Yes, I think he will," said Warner. "I've no reason to suppose he won't. I don't imagine that he left a perfectly good car here as a present for you, do you?"

"I dunno. I'm always a bit suspicious when the police want a chat with anyone. He gave his car a nasty biff, and I reckon it wasn't the gate post he hit. Some of them have got no consciences, you know, the way they'll bust another chap's outfit up and never stop to see if they've done him in or not."

"That's true enough," said Warner, seeing the direction of the other's thoughts. "Well, thanks for your assistance; when Mr. Ashe comes in for his Vauxhall, just let the Superintendent know on the q.t."

"Right, I'll see to it," replied Lecky.

Although Warner spent several hours more in Southampton, he did not succeed in learning anything further about the big fellow in a good grey Burberry, but he collected a lot of information about the vessels which had left Southampton on Monday, the 16th, and he interviewed the local police to enlist their assistance.

Going back to London by train, he considered the evidence he had acquired.

There had been no attempt at secrecy about the disposal of the Vauxhall, and that seemed quite reasonable. If Ashe had killed Lestrange, the former probably argued that there would not be any evidence to connect him with the murder. In that case he would doubtless return to England in good time, once he was satisfied that he was in no danger,—and claim his car. Warner could quite see the strength of Ashe's position. So far as it was possible to tell, no one had seen the Vauxhall approach Temple Grove, and no one could identify the corpse in Kirkham Barns.

The chief hope of connecting Ashe with the murder was to get him identified as James Merstham by one of his old acquaintances. The prosecution could then go on the assumption that Lestrange was Edward Merstham,—but it was far from being a clear case. The whole of the evidence was circumstantial—and a lot of it rested on pure guess work—and would have to remain at that.

"I wonder if it was the other way round," pondered Warner. "So far as the evidence goes, it can be twisted to point to two different conclusions, and can't I hear counsel for the defence airing Bond's ideas and trying to prove that Vivian Lestrange was simply the figment of Eleanor Clarke's imagination. Meanwhile, it's a case of wait and see, until Michael Ashe satisfies himself that it's safe to appear in public, or to write another book... It'll be too bad if we're to lose Ashe and Lestrange simultaneously, considering there's hardly a writer to compare with either of them on their own ground."

CHAPTER XIII

WARNER HAD ONLY JUST REACHED HIS OFFICE THE DAY after his visit to Southampton when Andrew Marriott called him up on the telephone.

"You seemed to have got a bee in your bonnet about Michael Ashe last time you were here," he said. "I thought you might be interested to know that I've just heard from him. His letter came from Genoa."

"Glory!" exclaimed Warner to himself, but to Marriott he said, "I'm delighted to hear it. I've been worrying over him a bit. Look here, may I come round and see his letter?"

"Certainly," replied Marriott, "but I'm afraid you won't be much enlightened; it's only about a slip in some proofs which he has just noticed."

"It's the fact that he has written at all which matters," said Warner. "Have you got the envelope which the letter came in?"

"Certainly I have."

"Then please take care of it," said Warner. "I'll be round within a few minutes."

When Warner was shown into Marriott's office the publisher looked at him with an air of amusement.

"Good morning, Chief Inspector," he said, "I was quite glad to get this letter from Ashe. You seemed to have got hold of an idea that he had disappeared for good. If that were his intention, he certainly would not have been writing to me about proof sheets. Here is his letter,—though as I told you, it is hardly likely to be of interest to you."

Warner took the sheet and studied it.

"Dear Marriott," ran the note. "I happened to be glancing through my spare proof of *Before the Mast*, and noticed another error which had escaped my notice before. On page 257, line 10, the word 'navigating' should be altered to 'navigation.' If this correction is too late for the first edition, you might see that later impressions are rectified. Yours, Michael Ashe."

There was neither address nor date on the letter, and it was scribbled on a piece of manuscript paper; the envelope showed the date of posting clearly. The stamp was an Italian one, and the cancelling imprint of "Genova 4-5-34" was perfectly clear.

"Now, I ask you," said Marriott plaintively, "would Ashe have written to me if he'd been intending to do a bolt? It's true that he hasn't put any address on his letter—that's typical of him—but the post mark's as clear as daylight."

"Yes," agreed Warner. "It certainly is. Now are you quite certain this letter is from Ashe? It is no forgery?"

Marriott sighed. "Do you think that writing would be easy to forge? I don't. In fact I'm prepared to swear that it isn't a forgery. Moreover, it refers to the proof sheets of his last book. Two proof copies are sent to the author, one of which, having been previously examined by a reader, is corrected again by the author and returned to us. The spare copy is kept by the author. No one but Ashe could have referred to the pagination of the proof copy because no one else has a copy of the proofs,—unless of course, you wish to extend your researches to the printers. The paper and envelope are similar to several which I have received from Ashe lately. In short, that is a letter from Ashe, and from no one else."

Warner examined the envelope again.

"Does he usually type his envelopes and not his letters?" he enquired, and Marriott replied.

"Sometimes both, sometimes neither. I'm afraid I'm not in the habit of keeping his envelopes, but I have several of his letters, if you care to see them."

Marriott opened a cabinet which stood in the corner of his room, and produced a file of letters. Warner, watching him, promptly said, "May I see one of the typed ones, too, please?"

Again the publisher agreed, and Warner put together two specimens, one a holograph, and one a typescript, saying, "I must ask you to let me have charge of these. Of course their contents will be treated as confidential, and they will be returned to you later."

Once again Marriott sighed. "Very well," he said, "I quite realise my protests will be quite futile, so I won't waste time formulating them, but I think you would be safe in taking my word for it that that letter is not a forgery."

"I'm quite sure it isn't," said Warner quietly. Something in the seriousness of his voice made the publisher turn and look at him in some concern.

"I have tried not to bother you with questions," he said, "but you must admit that I have a very real interest in this problem you're working at. Can you give me no idea of the course you are pursuing? Lestrange, for example?"

"I can answer that question quite straightforwardly," replied Warner. "Our researches into Vivian Lestrange's identity have not got us anywhere. Apart from surmise, I don't know anything more about him than I did when I first read the report of his disappearance. Bond, I might tell you, still treasures his theory that Eleanor Clarke is pulling the leg of the law, and although I don't agree with him, I have no proof either way. We have received a lot of anonymous letters—some rather original, but we're still groping."

"And it seems that your groping leads you in this direction?" said Marriott, rather tartly, pointing to the sheaf of letters in Warner's hand.

"It seems so," agreed the Chief Inspector, and then added "Say, if I put it like this. We know a crime has been committed, and the evidence leads us to suspect that Lestrange and Ashe are connected with that crime. What parts they played in it, I can't tell you, but I want to find them. It's to your interest that I should do so, moreover, for I think that you won't receive any more manuscripts from either of them till this case is cleared up."

"The two best sellers we've ever had!" groaned Marriott. "It's simply maddening!"

Leaving the sorrowful publisher shaking his head over the perverseness of fate, Warner hastened back to Scotland Yard in a fever to discover whether his powers of observation had played him false. Running up the steps to his room he unlocked a drawer, and produced the typescript letter sent by "A product of the penal system," and compared the typing with that of Ashe's letters and of the envelope with the Genoa post mark. Warner had made no mistake,—the typing, with its little irregularities due to a worn machine, was identical. Sitting back, the letters spread out before him, Warner lighted a cigarette and drew in a deep, comfortable breath of smoke as he leaned back in his chair and thought, sorting out his ideas into order.

His first impulse was to go to Genoa himself, and then he dismissed the idea as futile. He did not speak Italian, and he had never seen Michael Ashe. The Italian police, with the description he could send them, could do as much without him as they could if he were with them. Their system of registration of aliens was very thorough, as Warner knew, but even as he made arrangements for an interpreter and a clear line on the continental telephone system, Warner thought that the chances of catching his quarry were small. Genoa, of all places, with its network of communications by sea and land. That letter had been posted three days ago, and by now Ashe might be anywhere in Europe, in Africa, or even into Asia, or the Levant. He might have doubled back to England again, or have shipped on some cargo vessel bound for South America. If Staunton's story of Ashe's past adventures were true, the writer might have another personality all ready to hand, and a man who had sailed before the mast in a small trading ship in the Malay Archipelago would not be at loss in any port in the world.

Nevertheless, the net was spread. Under Warner's directions, by cable, wireless, and long distance telephone, a description of Michael Ashe found its way over the civilised world to police authorities and harbour authorities, to ships at sea and shipping agents in ports.

"One day telleth another and one night certifieth another," said Warner, remembering in a flash the analogy used in that anonymous letter. "I've made it as hot as I can for him, and that's that."

Resting from his labours over a cup of tea, Warner was told that a Mr. Vargon was asking for him, and he welcomed the diversion caused by the lawyer's unexpected visit.

"I'm jolly glad to see you, sir!" Warner exclaimed, when his visitor was shown in. "I've been having a hectic time of it the last few hours, but you've come at the right moment, when I've time for a breather. Tea? It's strong enough to poison you, I'm afraid, but they like their tea with a kick in it here."

"Good Gad! Not for me, I thank you," growled Vargon in his deep voice. "Too much respect for the only inside I'm likely to possess. I happened to have business in town, and I thought I'd look you up to tell you about a few enquiries I've been making about the Mersthams,—unless you've blown that theory sky-high by now."

"Not a bit," replied Warner. "In fact I'm counting on it as our main hope of arriving at a reasonable solution of the glorious muddle we seem to be wallowing in. You'd like to hear about proceedings since I saw you, so here goes."

The old lawyer listened with close attention to Warner's exposition, and read the famous Penal Product letter, his hooked eyebrows making an ever-acuter angle above his prominent nose, his jaw jutting out and his ears actually twitching in the intensity of his interest. When he had finally examined the letters from Michael Ashe, he handed back the papers to Warner saying,

"Well, you call it a glorious muddle. I should have thought you'd got evidence enough to call it a clear case."

"Meaning that Ashe killed Lestrange? It looks like it, but whether I've caught an attack of scepticism from Bond I don't know, but I'm still on the look-out for a leg-pull. One thing is perfectly certain,—the typewriter—a Corona portable—which Ashe used for his letters was also used by our 'Penal Product' correspondent."

"That's fool proof, isn't it?"

"The identity of the machine is indisputable, but more than one person could have worked the oracle. Take Marriott, the publisher. He could have cooked these earlier letters from Ashe, sent off the later ones equally easily and generally have manipulated the leg-pull. Not that I take that suspicion seriously, it's merely a habit to look at every side of a problem."

"How would you connect up Marriott and Kirkham Barns?"

"I can't,—for the present, and as I have told you, I'm counting on Kirkham to see us out of the wood. Let us reconsider this Merstham theory. We have two men, Ashe and Lestrange, who fit the descriptions of James and Edward Merstham. The probability is that Ashe is James and Lestrange is Edward. If Staunton is to be believed,—and he seemed very confident—Ashe was seafaring while Edward Merstham was in Parkhurst Gaol, so that settles which of them is which in their new characters. One thing has puzzled me considerably. Assuming that Ashe was James Merstham, why on earth did he ever go near his brother Edward? My first idea was that Ashe recognised something in the Lestrange books which told him that the author was brother Edward. Now the one person on earth whom Ashe should have avoided was his brother. Edward had every reason for seeking James, but not vice versa."

"Yes, there you're quite right,—unless James felt that he'd never be safe while Edward was still alive."

"Let sleeping dogs lie is a good motto,—but I have another theory on the subject. Ashe undoubtedly did a little sleuthing after Eleanor Clarke,—and perhaps that was his undoing. Imagine Ashe, having followed the trail to Temple Grove, forcing his way in, either by a ruse or by brute strength, in order to find out for himself the truth of the Lestrange story and then finding himself face to face with brother Edward. What a surprise for both of them!"

"Gad! Yes! You're right there!" barked Vargon. "It was a case of he who hesitates is lost. From what you've told me of him, Ashe isn't the type of man to indulge in second thoughts when he sees his own security threatened. He shot first and thought afterwards,—and his thinking must have been pretty comprehensive. The main puzzle is, what did he do about the housekeeper? It's the fact that he got her out of the way that makes me think the shooting wasn't so unpremeditated as you suggest. Your first idea that Ashe had tumbled to Lestrange's identity through the medium of his books is more convincing. He got rid of the housekeeper first and settled brother Edward next. That's vastly more probable to my thinking."

"But, damn it all! Ashe couldn't have believed Lestrange was brother Edward!" cried Warner. "Remember the early part of the story. Ashe went to Marriott, and asked him to arrange a dinner party so that he could meet Lestrange. I've only just seen the force of that, dolt that I am! If Ashe thought that Lestrange was his brother, would he have risked going to dine in another man's flat with the brother he'd left in the lurch, in the certainty that Edward would say, 'that man is a scoundrel and there's a warrant out against him. Send for the police.' Confound everything, is it likely?"

Vargon laughed. "Funny how slow one is to see an obvious point... If we could only have reversed the characters, and made

James into Lestrange, and Edward into Ashe, everything could have fitted perfectly."

"I'm practically certain that Ashe isn't Edward," said Warner. "The finger-print people have been working at the maps in Ashe's car, and at these letters. I admit it's a pretty rotten job for them. The maps are covered with smudges made by a man using driving gloves,—there isn't a clear print on them, and these letters have been handled by Marriott and his clerk till they're as hopeless as the maps, but they haven't got any trace of a print that resembles Edward's in the whole conglomeration. They've got several which may be Ashe's, but that doesn't get us anywhere. And again there's Staunton's evidence."

Vargon pulled one of his big ears thoughtfully.

"Yes, that complicates matters," he said, "but let's get back to Michael Ashe. That letter, certainly in his handwriting and posted in Genoa three days ago, indicates that the fellow is still alive, or was alive three days ago. I think you've got to take it as the most reasonable probability that Ashe went to Temple Grove, shot Lestrange, removed the body to Kirkham, and then drove down to Southampton and cleared out of the country to watch developments."

"That's a nice straightforward way of putting it," said Warner, "but let us consider the dates of our chief events. On Monday, 16th, Ashe's car was garaged at Southampton. On April 26th, a packet of Treasury notes was posted at the London General Post Office to Miss Clarke. On the evening of May 4th the letter from the 'Penal Product' was posted, also at the G.P.O. Yet on the evening of May 4th, Ashe's letter was posted in Genoa. The same typewriter was used for all these communications but the last two could not have been posted by *one* person."

"Yes. Now I see the complications," said Vargon thoughtfully, "but are you certain that that last letter of Ashe's was really posted in Genoa?"

"Our experts are pretty sound when it comes to detecting fakes," replied Warner. "They are satisfied that the stamp is genuine, and that the cancelling is genuine. That envelope went through the post at Genoa all right, and the stamp has not been tampered with. It was in the letter-box at Langston's this morning, and was probably delivered last night, after their office was closed. The times are all right, and the cancelling is all right. So far as human probability is concerned it came from Genoa. The handwriting is Michael Ashe's, the paper and envelope are similar to the ones he habitually uses; there are traces of fingerprints which coincide with traces on his other letters, and the typing on the envelope was done with the same machine which he used for earlier letters."

Vargon chuckled. "That seems pretty conclusive," he said. "It means that if Ashe himself is in Genoa, he got an accomplice to post the London letters,—or vice versa."

"It's enough to give you a sick headache," said Warner. "I've been visualising Ashe doing a Charley's Aunt stunt on the continental railways,—and as for where he is now, the Lord alone knows. As likely as not in London, tucked away in some private haunt of his own. I've done all I can for the moment to spread a net for him. Now what's your news? I'm just in the right frame of mind to be receptive to fresh impressions."

"Well, I thought I'd done some rather useful work, but in the light of what you say, it probably doesn't count for much," replied Vargon. "You see I was counting on Lestrange being James Merstham, and now that idea seems knocked on the head, my researches aren't very helpful,—but here's the story and you can judge for yourself... I've been making enquiries around Tintern where the Mersthams used to live. You've had the local police on the job, I know, but a man like myself can often get at a lot that the police would never hear about."

"I know," said Warner. "Quite a lot of people, country folk especially, fight shy of the police. They're always afraid they're going to be dragged into some trouble."

"That's it," nodded Vargon, "whereas they trust me. Now it appears that James Merstham had an affair with a woman who lived near Tintern, a farmer's daughter she was, about the same age as James and coming of respectable people. The village folk expected him to marry her, for though she wasn't of the gentry, to use their phrase, the father was pretty prosperous. Anyway there was a lot of talk about her; but she suddenly left the district without anyone knowing where she went to. Some people said that James was keeping her elsewhere, some said she'd gone away to save her face. It all happened soon after the war, but the woman—her name was Alice Latimer—has never been heard of since. Her father would never answer any question about her, and he's died since. You can see for yourself fast enough how I thought she could fit the story."

"As Mrs. Fife," replied Warner promptly. "This is getting more and more interesting. Wait a minute and see if we can make anything out of it." Leaning back in his chair, smoking furiously, Warner pondered with knitted brows, and at last said:

"How would this work? Let us disregard Staunton's evidence completely. Then we can go back to our original theory that Lestrange was James Merstham, carefully concealed because he knows a warrant is still out against him, and Michael Ashe is the avenging Edward. James, as Lestrange, settled down in Temple Grove with his old ladylove as housekeeper and Edward (as Michael Ashe) ran him to earth there... How does that fit?"

"You're still up against the same complication,—that of the housekeeper," objected Vargon. "You'll have to assume that Ashe decoyed Mrs. Fife away and disposed of her so completely that you have no traces of her at all, and then returned to finish off Lestrange. Whichever way you read the puzzle it looks as though you've got to trace a second murder before you get to the bottom of it."

For awhile both men pondered in silence; as Warner had said every fresh discovery seemed to make the tangle more complicated, and the elusive Lestrange refused to be fitted into any consistent part.

"Look here," said the lawyer at last, "I'm no good at detecting, but I've had a lot of experience in considering evidence. Let me set out the facts on paper in my own way and see if I can make any sense of them. First of all we'll have a list of persons involved in the case. You can dictate, I'll set it down."

"Right," said Warner with a twinkle. "I'm well up in the task."

At the end of several minutes, Vargon read through his list.

Personalia.

1. *Vivian Lestrange.* No evidence concerning him save that given by,
2. *Eleanor Clarke.* Very little known about her save what she herself has stated.
3. *Mrs. Fife.* A woman of about fifty. Terse, business-like and not badly educated.

4. *Andrew Marriott*. Well known as a publisher, highly respected; his interests coincide with the continued output of Lestrange's and Ashe's novels.

5. *Michael Ashe*. Only known to the public through the medium of his novels.

Practical Evidence.

1. Possible bullet hole in window of Temple Grove.
2. Corpse at Kirkham, with bullet from ·45 pistol in the brain and pocket-book on person.
3. Parcel of Treasury Notes. ⎫
4. Penal Product Letter. ⎬ Similar typing
5. Ashe's Letter from Genoa. ⎭
6. Ashe's car, with road maps of Hereford, left at Southampton.

"Now all that is concrete evidence except point 1, section 1," said Warner. "One has to admit in justice to Bond, that the existence of the man Vivian Lestrange, is based on Eleanor Clarke's evidence. Regard that as suspect and you find yourself faced with the most fantastic possibilities. Now it's plain on the face of it that Eleanor Clarke is the connecting link with all the other characters. Look for yourself."

"Eleanor Clarke knows—or knew—Lestrange, Mrs. Fife, Andrew Marriott and Michael Ashe," said Vargon.

"Exactly. The whole boiling of them. Now two questions presented themselves at the outset of the case. First, the disappearance of the housekeeper. Second, in the event of foul play, why was Miss Clarke not informed by telephone that she could take a holiday? The answer to the last query is that the plotters wanted the police informed,—and that argument holds whether Miss Clarke is in the plot or not. Now still basing my idea strictly on the evidence, here is fantastic surmise number one. Michael Ashe is at the bottom of the whole thing. He wrote under two names, one Vivian Lestrange, one Michael Ashe. With the connivance of Mrs. Fife and Miss Clarke, he established the mythical identity of Vivian Lestrange, and when the time was ripe, he proceeded to commit a murder under cover of the said Lestrange, the latter providing an identity for the corpse.

"In that case," said Vargon, "Eleanor Clarke is an accessory."

"Not necessarily to murder," retorted Warner. "Her help may have been enlisted on the lines of hoaxing the police in order to study their methods at close quarters. Don't look so disgusted, sir! It's a most picturesque idea. Eleanor Clarke (pretending to be Lestrange) praises Michael Ashe to Marriott. Ashe praises Lestrange. Sequel, a dinner party, at which legs are pulled all round and much astonishment is simulated. Later, Ashe arranges for his private murder, and instructs the housekeeper to vanish, and Eleanor Clarke to inform the police of Lestrange's disappearance. You may look incredulous, but it's a theory which can be made to fit, assuming that both women are sufficiently devoted to Ashe, or sufficiently well paid by him. Eleanor Clarke is an unusual type. She has few friends and no relations. She would have been ideal for the part. Her job is a genuine typist's and secretary's job, and Temple Grove is kept up as a convenient retreat to which Ashe can retire at intervals."

Vargon chuckled. "It's a clever notion, but a bit too fantastic for me. It involves chucking the Merstham idea overboard, too…"

"Not at all," countered Warner. "Ashe would fit the part of either brother and Alice Latimer becomes Mrs. Fife."

Vargon returned to his list of evidence, as a drowning man might clutch at a life-buoy.

"Imagination's not in my line," he growled. "Studying this list, I'd say that there was a possibility that any—or all—of them may be involved, but I'd be disposed to rule out Marriott. He's a successful business man whose life has been open and above board, and I don't see how he could profit by games of this kind. An advertisement's one thing, murder's another. However, it's obvious that Ashe is involved, and probably one of the others with him. You know you've changed flags since last we met; you were all in favour of Eleanor Clarke's innocence then."

"I know," replied Warner. "I would still say—on my own judgment—that she has told the truth, but everyone's judgment is fallible, and the more I consider the evidence the more I realise that she is a contact with all our other evidence. You never know what a woman will do if she's in love, for instance, and she may be in love with Michael Ashe,—but let's get back to firmer ground. You said just now, 'advertisement's one thing, murder's another.' I'm going to apply that reasoning to Eleanor Clarke."

"In what way?"

"Tell her a few of the facts of the case. Going on Bond's assumption that Eleanor Clarke is working a leg-pull, and my own suggestion being that Michael Ashe is behind the leg-pull, it may be that Eleanor Clarke is only guilty of hoaxing the police. She may still think the whole thing is a joke. I'm going to tell her in plain words that the joke is a cover for murder."

"You argue that she's been used as a tool by the murderer, herself acting in ignorance of the murder, but supporting the bluff?"

"That's the idea."

"Well, I'll leave you to it," said Vargon. "On my reading of the probabilities, I should say that Lestrange and Ashe are the Merstham brothers, that Ashe shot Lestrange, and that you'll find the corpse of the housekeeper before you're out of the wood."

"In that case you've got to count Eleanor Clarke in as an accessory, in order to account for the posting of the letters," said Warner.

"Maybe, but not of necessity. There's nothing in giving anyone a letter to post. Ashe may have handed his Genoa letter to one of his sea-going pals with the request that it be posted in Genoa. There's one small crumb of comfort for you, Ashe will bob up again some time, provided you don't publish your suspicions about him. He's tried to impress you with the fact that Vivian Lestrange is dead by writing that 'Penal Product' letter, but the name Michael Ashe is a good paying proposition."

"Yes. I realise that," said Warner. "If I put the newspapers on to the Ashe story, it's a hundred to one chance against our ever seeing him again. He's had too long to get clear in."

"Meanwhile I'll leave you to invent some more fantastic explanations," chuckled Vargon. "That last one of yours was a good one."

"It was a damned good one," agreed Warner. "It explains a whole lot and fits in with odd bits of evidence… Before I tax my brain with further original efforts at reconstruction, I am going to have another shot at the competent Miss Clarke and just test her reactions to some of my little theories."

CHAPTER XIV

WARNER'S INTENDED VISIT TO ELEANOR CLARKE WAS delayed by the arrival of a report from the A.A. authorities concerning Michael Ashe's car,—the green Vauxhall Cadet which had been garaged at Southampton.

Immediately after he had left Lecky's garage, Warner had issued a description of the Vauxhall to the police and to the automobile clubs, in the hope that he would get a report to explain the damage done to the car, which certainly appeared to have been in some sort of minor collision. Warner hoped that by tracing the journey of the Vauxhall he might gain some light on Ashe's movements during the week-end of Lestrange's disappearance, but the news which was supplied by the A.A. caused the Chief Inspector to wonder if he had been wrong in indulging in fantastic surmises, and whether Vargon would not prove to be right in his opinion that this was going to be a straightforward case, with Ashe as the criminal. The report which had just arrived certainly suggested that Ashe had undertaken a journey in his car in the direction of Ross. It ran as follows:

The Vauxhall AB7469X had been seen on the main London–Cheltenham road, on the stretch between Burford and Northleach, shortly before one o'clock on the night of Sunday, April 15th, or to put it more precisely, on the very early morning of Monday, the 16th. Two young men had been returning to Northleach after spending the evening in Oxford, and their

route was along the Cheltenham road. They were travelling on
a motor cycle, one riding on the pillion seat, and they had come
to grief through swerving to avoid a tramp who had lurched out
suddenly into the road. The cycle struck a telegraph post, and the
lad on the pillion seat, Martin by name,—had been thrown clear
and was very little injured, but the driver of the cycle—named
Thomson—had struck his head against the post and lay uncon-
scious after the spill. They were on a lonely piece of road, and
Martin was frantic with anxiety, not knowing whether to leave
his friend in order to get help from the nearest habitation, or
to stay with him in the hope of assistance arriving in the shape
of another vehicle. There was but little traffic on the road at
that hour but to Martin's relief a car was heard approaching,
and the lad stood in the middle of the road, signalling in the
hope of stopping the car and getting help. The driver slowed
down,—as he had to—for with the wreckage of the cycle, which
had rebounded into the road, and the positions of Martin and
the tramp, there was not much room for him to pass.

"I say, we've had a smash," shouted Martin to the driver as
the car slowed down, but to the lad's surprise, the driver did not
pull up. Jumping on the running board, Martin shouted through
the window,

"My pal's half done in, I only want you to give him a lift to
the doctor's."

The only reply was, "Get off!"

"Damn it! You can't leave a chap to die by the road," protested
Martin, and once again was answered,

"Get out! Get off that running board, or I'll make you!"

Since the car was accelerating and Martin did not want
to leave his friend alone by the road, he jumped clear, but he

managed to get the number of the car because he had confused notions of "getting the law on the driver" for refusing aid under such circumstances.

The A.A. scout who drove up a little later and who proved a friend in need, tried to explain to Martin that "you can't have the law on a man" for refusing to stop on a main road after midnight, but the scout took the number of the car to report to his own organisation, in case witnesses were required in the event of Thomson's death. Thomson having recovered, no steps were taken in the matter.

The car was correctly described by Martin—a green Vauxhall, saloon body. The driver was a fairly big man, clean-shaven, "not a young man, but not very old" was all that Martin would hazard in the way of description—but it would do for Ashe.

"And now we can begin to make a plan of his route," said Warner to himself with some satisfaction. "One can assume that he drove from London, and see how it works out."

It worked out quite satisfactorily. Taking the point where the Vauxhall was seen and the time given, Warner made out a time table which seemed to fit the case. The best route from London to Ross was by way of Oxford, Cheltenham and Gloucester, and the Vauxhall was seen on the Oxford to Cheltenham road between Burford and Northleach at 12.45 a.m. on Monday morning. Reckoning on the clear roads an average speed of thirty miles an hour seemed reasonable, which gave the following time table:

London. 10.0 p.m. Sunday evening.
Oxford. Midnight.
Burford. 12.40 a.m. Monday.
Northleach. 1.0 a.m. Monday.

Cheltenham. 1.30 a.m. Monday.
Gloucester. 1.50 a.m. Monday.
Ross. 2.40 a.m. Monday.

With this timing as a rough guide, Warner reckoned that the
Vauxhall could have reached Dick Barton's cottage by the river
at 3 a.m., and allowing an hour and a half for the activities of
moving the corpse and disposing of it, the driver could have
regained his car by 4.30 a.m. while it was still dark and long before
the earliest of the farm hands would be stirring.

Once again Warner turned to his road maps. The Vauxhall
had been garaged in Southampton on Monday morning—but
there was plenty of time for the journey from Ross. Assuming
that the route chosen was via Gloucester, Cirencester, Swindon,
Andover and Winchester—a distance of a little under a hundred
miles, the driver of the Vauxhall would have had plenty of
time for breakfast *en route*,—and, as Warner reminded himself,
"even if a man's committed a murder, he's still got to have
something to eat, for he couldn't drive a car straight if he
fasted too long."

Here then was an explanation which fitted the facts. Ashe
had driven to Temple Grove, shot Lestrange, put his body into
the car and driven to Ross. After that he had gone straight to
Southampton and taken a boat for the continent. Since nearly
three weeks had elapsed without any sign of a police enquiry
moving in his direction, he had considered it safe to write to
Marriott in the normal way of business, indicating that he was
taking a holiday in the Mediterranean as he had suggested. The
next step was to discover who was acting as accomplice in the
matter of posting the letters.

Once again Warner fell into a brown study, marshalling the facts of the case in his mind. Ashe was far from being a fool, and he would certainly have counted on the fact that the "Penal Product" letter would have been closely examined, and that the packet sent to Eleanor Clarke would be similarly treated, yet it evidently had not occurred to him that the police would examine his correspondence with Marriott. Putting himself into Ashe's place, Warner tried to think out what fears he himself would have had that a connecting link might be forged between the two writers. There was that dinner party,—but even if the police had been told of it, they couldn't have assumed that thereby Ashe learned anything of Lestrange. He had only met the secretary. As for the matter of tracing the taxi man who had told Ashe Eleanor Clarke's address, why should the police think of such a step?

At this stage in his conjectures, Warner banged the ashes out of his pipe with a feeling of exasperation.

"Damn it! the man's a fool! He's simply asking to be hanged, behaving like a simpleton... Or am I the simpleton? Why didn't he buy a new typewriter or use somebody else's?"

Once again the telephone bell rang,—this time it was the Winchester police, with further evidence to reinforce the theory that Ashe and his Vauxhall had done exactly what Warner had assumed.

Intensive enquiry on the part of the rural police force had elicited the information that the Vauxhall had been in collision with a farm waggon between Andover and Winchester at 8 o'clock on Monday, April 16th. The driver of the waggon had been to blame for not controlling his horse properly; the horse had shied at the car as the two vehicles rounded a corner; the car had been well in to the left, but as the horse bolted forward the heavy wheel had caught the wing and running board of the car. When the farm hand had got his horse under control again and come back to interview the driver of the car, he had expected trouble, knowing the collision to have been his own fault. As it turned out the driver of the car, who had alighted to inspect the damage, contented himself with swearing at the waggoner as a drunken oaf, and had then got back into the Vauxhall saying that he had not the time to stop and argue. On both occasions when the Vauxhall had been observed,—Warner meditated,—the driver had done just what Ashe might have been expected to do under similar circumstances,—gone on as quickly as possible and probably hoped that his car had not been carefully noted by those with whom he came into contact.

"Well, he may be a damned fine writer, and may be good at picturesque and anonymous letters, but he's a thundering careless devil," growled Warner to himself. "We ought to catch him if he's as silly as that…"

But would it be so easy? Ashe, with his knowledge of seafaring, might be the hardest person in the world to come up with. He would know the ropes in all the ports, know exactly how to dodge from one place to another, and he probably had a dozen convenient hiding places to conceal himself in. The name "Michael Ashe" might be but one of half a dozen different aliases.

Just as he was about to reach for his hat to pursue his intention of visiting Eleanor Clarke, Warner stood stock still. Another notion had come into his head,—so simple that he was amazed that he had not thought of it before. He stood motionless in the middle of the room, his face screwed up in the intensity of his concentration, his eyes staring at the opposite wall unseeingly, while he murmured to himself, "Holy Moses! but that might fit." He was still standing thus rapt in his great idea, when a knock heralded the advent of Inspector Bond. When he entered, Warner, still in the throes of his new idea, gazed at him unknowingly until Bond said,

"Good day, sir. I've been thinking."

Warner burst out laughing.

"So have I," he retorted, "and my thoughts were long, long thoughts, as the poetry book has it. The upshot of them is to suggest that this case will never be solved by me, even though I'm willing to swear I've thought my way to the bottom of it. It's these nom-de-plumes that are our trouble, Bond,—double personality business and all that. If I petitioned Parliament do you think I could get an enactment that no man writes under any name but his own, and his finger-prints be registered on the title page?"

"No, sir, I don't," replied Bond dryly. "I'm told that some of 'em write under as many as six different names,—crimes as A, romances as B, fairy tales as C, belles-lettres as D, costume novels as E, and economics as F."

"It oughtn't to be allowed," groaned Warner. "Hardened offenders... recidivists, I call 'em. What's your news, Bond? Tell me something fresh. I keep on making re-arrangements of the same pieces, and every explanation I arrive at seems to work,— only I don't know which is the right one."

"That's just it," said Bond. "It's the same with me. I've been going over the same ground until I'm obsessed with it. I think Lestrange, I dream Lestrange, and I all but eat Lestrange. I can tell you what he—or she—paid in income tax, paid in rent and rates, paid in wages and housekeeping. I've had all the trades-men's books in and I've been through them with my missus."

"My hat!" said Warner, "that was a brain wave!"

"I wanted to know if enough food was provided in that house for one man and one and a half women," went on Bond. "That's why I brought my missus into it. She's a good housekeeper. Well, they spent on an average £4 a week in Temple Grove including beer and wine. I doubt if Mrs. Fife and Miss Clarke (who was only there to an occasional middle-day meal and tea) would have put away that amount of grub. They liked good food,—chicken and game occasionally, salmon and asparagus in season, but my wife tells me the shopping was carefully done—no silly extravagances. She found Mrs. Fife's cookery book in the kitchen, and made a note of the recipes marked. Between us we could tell you just what Lestrange liked to eat—devilled kidneys, curried prawns, pigeon pie, sole cooked in white wine..."

"Well, that doesn't sound like a couple of women!" said Warner.

"No," said Bond with a sigh. "If they ate all that they must have had good appetites,—but it's not impossible," he added firmly, "not if they were out to create an effect of having a man there. Then there's another thing I can tell you. Since that corpse turned up I've managed to make the bank manager see sense, and I've been through Lestrange's account for the last three years. There's a lot of money unaccounted for. Lestrange cashed big cheques pretty regularly; the upkeep of that house and such outgoings as wages and income tax didn't cost him half the income he made as a writer. The balance was either spent in some way we can't fathom or transferred elsewhere;—quite a tidy little sum, several thousands in all."

"Paid in blackmail, separate establishment, or a private nest egg?" queried Warner.

Bond shrugged his shoulders.

"Whichever way you look at it, sir," he went on in his careful way, "you've got the problem of the missing housekeeper. Now if Miss Clarke's at the back of all this hokey-pokey, I reckon the housekeeper's in it with her. If Miss Clarke's told the truth and Lestrange was murdered, I'm still disposed to think that the housekeeper was an accessory. Now where is she? You just suggested a separate establishment. How would it be if Mrs. Fife had retired to some place where she'd previously established another identity? Some niche into which she could slip without questions being asked about her as a stranger?"

"That's sound enough," admitted Warner, "but the devil of it is that there's nothing for us to get hold of."

"There's this," said Bond, and he produced from his pocket the most disreputable toothbrush Warner had ever seen.

"Go on," said the Chief Inspector. "I know you too well to suspect you of indulging in leg-pulls."

"Well, I argued this way," said Bond. "If Mrs. Fife had been doing a double personality stunt, the only time she had to do it was during the summer holidays when we know Temple Grove was shut up. Maybe she had a little house or a flat somewhere, and went to stay there during the holidays. I know it's just guessing," he admitted shamefacedly, but Warner cut in,

"Damn it, I've done nothing but guess. It was the only way in this blighted rigmarole. Go on!"

"It seemed to me that Mrs. Fife would have been almighty careful not to leave any traces of her private retreat," went on Bond, "but now and again, when one goes for a holiday, one brings home some oddment without noticing, so to speak, and you find it years afterwards and say, 'Why, I bought that at

Bognor.' I hoped for something of that kind which might have been overlooked in that grand clearing up at Temple Grove. I tell you," said Bond with a sudden burst of excitability, "I hunted in that qualified house until I was nearly demented. There isn't an article in it I haven't examined… and then at last I looked into every tin and pot, and among the cleaning things I found the silver polishing outfit, with whitening and what not, and that toothbrush,—used like my missis uses her old ones for brushing in the whitening." Bond paused and picked up the derelict toothbrush. "It was a good brush once," he said. "It's got the chemist's name on, see?—it was bought in Meads Street, Eastbourne."

"Bravo, Bond!" said Warner, and the other suddenly laughed aloud.

"I like to think of that dame tidying the house and seeing to it that there wasn't one blessed thing to give her away!" he said, with more enthusiasm in his voice than Warner had ever heard in it before. "She was so almighty careful. And, I ask you," he demanded, "if she or Lestrange didn't buy that toothbrush in Eastbourne, how did it get into that house? I can't see Miss Clarke bringing along her old toothbrushes to give to the housekeeper for cleaning silver, and, bar Miss Clarke, no outsider has been in that house. They didn't have a charwoman. Now since I was looking for some indication of where Mrs. Fife may have tucked herself away, don't you think I'm justified in guessing Eastbourne?"

"I certainly do," said Warner, and Bond went on.

"And here's another point. When I went and saw Miss Clarke about that packet of Treasury notes, she asked me off her own bat to search her rooms, to see if I could find a typewriter there…"

"What a sensible woman that one is," murmured Warner, and Bond got red in the face.

"Yes, by jing!" he said wrathfully. "She always does the right thing. What is it the French say—gives you 'le cafard.' That's what she gives me. The proper pip, I call it, in my own lingo. Well, sir, I didn't say no when she asked me to have a 'look-see,' although I knew well enough I shouldn't find the typewriter there, but I looked at things pretty carefully."

"I bet you did!" interpolated Warner, and Bond continued.

"Everything was as neat as could be, just what you'd expect to find in the flat of a cultured female, nothing else, but I noted one thing for future reference. Slipped into an ordinary A.B.C. time-table I found a couple of photographs,—just small unmounted snaps, and it's not until today I've found out what they represented. They're both photographs of the old church at the back of Eastbourne,—Old Town church they call it, and an old pub called The Lamb nearby."

The two men looked at one another in silence for a second or so, and then Warner said,

"And you figure it out that Mrs. Fife is living in retirement at Eastbourne in some nook previously arranged by herself and Miss Clarke?"

"It's a possibility, that's all I suggest," said Bond. "We've so little to go on in this case that we're driven to sheer guess work."

"And now let's see how our guesses accommodate themselves to the facts we've acquired this morning," said Warner, and recapitulated for Bond's benefit the facts concerning the typewriter, the Genoa letter, and the Vauxhall car.

Bond's face expressed something ridiculously like disappointment.

"Michael Ashe," he growled. "These writers, they're a nice lot!—but where do you think Mrs. Fife is in all this caboodle?"

"I'd have two guesses," replied Warner. "One, she may be concealed in a lonely grave. Two, she's in Eastbourne,—and I'd give it as my opinion that the latter is the more probable. Most likely she's living comfortably as Mrs. Jones or Mrs. Robinson,—a worthy dame who has stayed in the same place as before and is taken for granted."

"Then you reckon she's in with Ashe?" demanded Bond, adding eagerly, "And what about our Miss Clarke?"

"Ah!" said Warner, "now we're back at our original riddle. So far as she is concerned, you have been quite consistent all the way through,—you believed at the outset that she was conceal-ing the real facts of the case and you still believe it. I'm afraid that I have been less consistent. I believed in her to begin with; she seemed straightforward and perfectly natural, and the story she told hung together. Since then, as I have seen how she's tied up with every part of our case, knowing all the characters so to speak, I've begun to emulate Thomas. I thought at first she was so natural in her obvious concern for her employer—'that kind old boy' she called him,—and now I'm wondering if her concern wasn't really applied to Michael Ashe,—a woman's tendency to protect the man she's in love with, no matter what he's done. I still can't tell which impulse is the right one, and I've made up so many variations to account for the facts that I'm ashamed to give expression to them... I wonder if Miss Clarke could be bluffed, Bond?"

"If you want my opinion on that point, I'd say 'no' every time, sir," growled Bond. "She's one of the people who doesn't give anything away."

"I wonder," said Warner. "Remember that we haven't told her anything of our recent discoveries. That Kirkham business didn't leak into the London Press, because the local men were so careful over the way they produced their evidence. Eleanor Clarke couldn't know about the discovery of the corpse unless she'd had a local paper, and she wouldn't have risked having one sent to her. Say if I tried a reconstruction of the story on her, leaving out names. I might describe how the shooting took place at Temple Grove, the moving of the body in the Vauxhall, the planting it in the cottage and so forth, and then leap on her the fact that Mrs. Fife is living quietly at Eastbourne. If she's involved in the crime, I reckon she'd have a shot at warning Mrs. Fife. She might give herself away if we watched her carefully."

Bond shrugged his shoulders.

"I suppose there is something in the idea, sir," he said, "though I can picture her sitting listening as demure as a cat, expressing consternation as the story progressed, and finally inviting you to read all the letters in her blotter, and search her bureau just to safeguard herself."

Warner laughed. "It's funny to think how one person's manner can affect other people so differently. The very coolness of her logical mind made me believe her and you disbelieve her. Well, here's for it. I'm going to ring her up and find out if she's at home, to save me trapesing out to Clare Court for nothing."

"Well, I only hope you find her all right when you want her," said Bond. "Every morning when I wake up I wonder if we shan't be told she's made off. It's all very well to say she's being shadowed, but it's no use pretending that that's infallible, sir. It's fairly easy to keep a person under observation for a limited period, but when it runs into weeks, it's a different matter.

The watcher tires,—gets accustomed to the job and develops a blind spot."

"Yes, there's something in that," agreed Warner, "also I believe that if a woman like Eleanor Clarke used her brains she could outwit a watcher and get away pro tem,—but that doesn't mean she'd find it easy to remain hidden. In any case, I don't think she intends to bolt; guilty or innocent, her cue all along has been to sit tight and try to appear helpful."

Taking up the receiver, Warner put through a call and a moment later he smiled cheerfully at Bond.

"She's there all right. Now for the dramatic exposition that bounces her off her balance!"

"You're an optimist, you are, sir," said Bond.

CHAPTER XV

WHEN WARNER RECEIVED NO REPLY TO HIS RING AT THE door of Eleanor Clarke's flat, he gave a slight whistle and then rang again. Still receiving no answer, he walked down the stairs to the entrance hall in a thoughtful frame of mind, intending to find the door porter, but by the time the Chief Inspector reached ground level he saw a figure he recognised,—Farling, the C.I.D. man, whose duty it was to keep Miss Clarke under observation, and the expression on the face of the shadower told its own tale.

"I've lost her, sir," said Farling, in the tone of one who realises that he has been weighed in the balance and found wanting, but Warner did not waste time on rebukes.

"Tell me about it quickly," he said, "She was at home forty minutes ago."

"Yes, sir. She came out at half past one, and turned to the right, walking quite leisurely. I followed her to Holly Walk, that's a quiet little road about five minutes from here. She has been there before, I think she's got a friend at No. 14. Anyway, she went in there and rung the bell. I waited a few doors off. Next minute a taxi passed me, and she ran down the steps again just as it drew up, jumped in and was off straight away. I couldn't do anything, there was no hope of another taxi, and there wasn't a car or a van anywhere near. I got the taxi's number, but that was all I could do. He was round the corner in a brace of shakes."

"It can't be helped," said Warner, "that's the sort of thing which is always likely to happen in a job like yours. You'd better find out about the different taxi ranks and trace the driver. How long ago was it when you lost sight of her?"

"Not more than ten minutes, sir."

Warner thought hard. When he had talked to Eleanor Clarke over the 'phone she had simply said "All right. Will you come along now, that will suit me quite well," and she had immediately set about this scheme of ridding herself of the watchdog whom Warner had explained was detailed to guard her against possible dangers! And where was she going? It was natural that, lacking any other suggestion, Warner's mind turned to Bond's story and his suggestion of a retreat in Eastbourne. At least it was worth trying. Nothing else could be done in the way of tracing Eleanor Clarke until the taxi driver was found,—and Warner guessed that his evidence was not likely to be very helpful. Eleanor Clarke was much too intelligent to have used the taxi for much more than a quick get away. Turning to Farling, Warner said, "Get out an all stations call for that taxi man. They'll pass it on to the point duty men and he'll be found quickest that way. Then you can try the local ranks. If you get any news, telephone to the Yard and to Inspector Bond. All reports to be sent to the Yard—I'll keep in touch with them myself."

Using the telephone in the porter's lobby, Warner rang up Bond and told him what had happened. Bond grunted. "Just what I expected, sir," he said.

"Issue a general warning and description," said the Chief Inspector, "I'll ring you again later."

Turning to Farling after he had telephoned, Warner said, "How was she dressed, and had she got a bag?"

"No bag—barring a little hand bag, sir. Navy blue costume, small navy blue hat, grey stockings, black shoes."

"H'm. Neat and not noticeable," said Warner. "Get on the job after that taxi and report the minute you learn anything. She may come back after all."

A few minutes later Warner was in a taxi on his way to Victoria Station. He hadn't much belief in what he was doing, but it seemed worth while. If there were anything in the Eastbourne idea (and the evidence for it was so slight that Warner could have laughed at his own action in putting any faith in it) there was just a chance that Eleanor Clarke might have determined to slip away and hide in the hypothetical ménage in Eastbourne. That being so, she would probably go straight to the station and get a train before Warner would have time to stop her.

Glancing at his watch, Warner saw that it was only twenty minutes since Farling had seen his charge drive off in the taxi, but Warner was pretty sure that Eleanor Clarke would have dropped her taxi at some convenient point near a 'bus stop or tube station. After that she would probably take some indirect route to her destination. If she intended to go to Eastbourne, Victoria Station was her best terminus. At this hour of the day it was much more crowded than London Bridge, and she was more likely to escape notice. Once again Warner laughed to himself.

"Talk about following a will o' the wisp. Clues probable and otherwise—an elderly toothbrush and a couple of snaps!"

Nevertheless as Warner's taxi drove into Victoria Station yard, he caught sight of Eleanor Clarke herself. She had just alighted from a number 16 'bus, and she was watching for an opportunity to cross from the omnibus parking place to the booking office.

Just as Warner saw her, Eleanor Clarke averted her head and turned quickly back among the 'buses again.

"Damn!" said Warner, "she's seen me." Paying his taxi man, he raced across the station yard, but by the time he had dodged through the 'buses, his quarry had disappeared,—she had evidently succeeded in jumping on to a 'bus which had just gone through the south gates of the yard on its outward journey. Racing round the corner to the junction of Victoria Street, Warner saw the 'bus—a number 25—disappearing to the left of Grosvenor Gardens. Instead of pursuing it, Warner rushed back across the station yard to the gates on the north side, in time to see the 25 'bus re-appear as it swung into the "roundabout" of Grosvenor Gardens.

"But the Lord was not in the whirlwind," murmured Warner to himself. His alert lady had slipped off the 'bus just as he lost sight of it.

"Well, no one could want a better ground for hide and seek than this one," said Warner, as he walked past the shops which backed on to the station yard. There were three entrances to the yard itself, as well as the entrance to the underground with its subway leading up into the station; there was the Grosvenor Hotel with its own entrance both to street and station, to say nothing of the gates in the Buckingham Palace Road and the entrance to the continental side.

Warner decided to waste no further time in playing hide and seek among the multitudinous exits and entries to the Southern Railway. Instead he decided to concentrate on the next train to Eastbourne. Eleanor Clarke's appearance at Victoria Station seemed to indicate that Bond's toothbrush and snap-shots were the trump cards in the case.

There was a train to Eastbourne at 3.10, and Warner decided
that he had better watch the approach to the platform from some
place where he would be himself concealed. The train would
start from No. 16 platform and the barrier was just beside the
entrance to the Buckingham Palace Road. He had a few minutes
in which to enlist assistance from the station police and to give
a description of the neat blue-clad figure he had seen mounting
the 'bus in the station yard. Finally, when he concealed himself
in the shadowy doorway of the Custom's office, facing the barrier to No. 16 platform, Warner felt that his chance of seeing his
quarry was very slight. It was just bad luck that Eleanor Clarke
had caught sight of him,—as he was certain she had—when he
alighted from his taxi.

It was just before three o'clock when he saw her again,
dressed now in a light rain coat and a soft felt hat. But for Warner
there was no possibility of not recognising the clear-cut profile
he saw as she hurried along the platform which ran parallel with
that of No. 16. Warner was out of his doorway like a shot. At
No. 15 platform stood the Brighton train, a non-stop starting
at 3.0 o'clock. He had just time to race through the barrier by
which the taxis emerged, and he saw Eleanor Clarke jump on to
the Brighton train just as it was signalled to start. Jumping in to
the nearest compartment actually as the train moved, Warner
watched from his window lest she should alight at the last
possible second and leave him in the lurch,—but as the electric
train accelerated he saw the whole length of platform, and no
Eleanor Clarke alighted.

With a sigh of relief Warner went out into the corridor and
walked back to the guard's van. From the guard he received con-
firmation of what he already knew,—the train was a non-stop,

due to make the journey in an hour, and no one could alight from it till it pulled up at Brighton.

Showing his card to the guard, Warner asked the man for his help. He showed him a photograph of Eleanor Clarke (a very good one which Bond had achieved on his own account) and asked him to go up the train and find where the lady was seated. A few minutes later the guard came back.

"She's in the front coach, sir. You'll have no trouble in getting her."

"I don't want to get her," replied Warner, "I want to follow her. Is there any means by which I can get a wire through to Brighton, so that one of the local men may be there and have a car ready?"

The guard pondered. "I'll tell you what I can do, sir. I can drop a letter to the station-master on to the platform as we run through Three Bridges. I'll work it so that one of the platform men will see the letter all right and then the station-master will ring through to Brighton and give any message that's necessary."

"Good. That will do excellently," replied Warner, and busied himself with a letter explaining who he was and what he wanted.

As the train ran into Brighton, Warner walked up the corridor of the train (with the guard in front of him lest they met Eleanor Clarke face to face), and the Chief Inspector stood inside the compartment immediately behind that one in which she sat. As the train drew up, Warner saw her go to the window, open the door and jump out on to the platform running as though for a race. He followed her through the barrier as close as he dared; instead of making for the exit, she turned sharp to the left and ran across the booking-hall parallel with the platform barriers.

There was a considerable crowd just outside the barrier, and Warner had his work cut out to slip through the crowd after her; he had no time to look out for the local detective who was presumably waiting for him by the ticket collector, for Eleanor Clarke could run like a hare, and Warner's one idea was to let her run without suspecting that she was being followed—once she saw him he knew his chase would be fruitless. To arrest her without any further evidence of guilt than merely giving him the slip would not help him at all.

Arrived at the extreme left of the station, she turned on to another platform and jumped into a train that was standing there, just as the guard blew his whistle. Warner tumbled into the final compartment and the small train steamed out of Brighton without the Chief Inspector having the least notion of whither he was travelling. His compartment being empty, he had to rely on the map on the wall opposite to give him an idea of his possible destination. He was soon satisfied that he had guessed what lay behind the energetic lady's manœuvres—this train was bound from Brighton to Lewes, and the latter was a junction through which ran all the Eastbourne trains.

Warner leaned back and smoked a cigarette, and thought how annoyed his Brighton colleague would be. Warner's orders in his letter from the train had been "A man to wait at the barrier, but not to do anything until he was ordered." Well, it was a good thing the Brighton man had stood by his orders: if two men had raced after her, Miss Clarke would certainly have observed them—Warner, being light of foot, hoped that he had followed unnoticed.

The long hideous rows of dreary grey houses which disfigure the downs immediately at the back of Brighton were soon left behind and the little train puffed its way through the rolling downland, the engine seeming to pant as it dragged up the ascent and plunged through smoky tunnels. Then Warner, seeing the ruined bastions of an ancient wall, knew that they were running into Lewes. Cautiously he watched the few passengers who got out,—but by no stretch of the imagination could one of them be recognised as Eleanor Clarke. Paying for his ticket, once again Warner took counsel with the guard of the train,—a sensible fellow who undertook to examine the tickets of all the passengers on the train. Once again Warner was assured that he had not lost his quarry, she was safely in the train, two coaches in front of him.

"Where does this train go next?" demanded Warner.

"Newhaven and Seaford, sir," replied the guard.

Warner sat back in his seat, giving vent to a whistle. Newhaven Harbour!—was he going to follow the elusive lady on to the cross-channel steamer, and so on to Genoa after all?

Sitting in the noisy little train, running across the wide river meadows between Lewes and Newhaven, Warner felt disgusted with himself. Had Bond been right all along in his conviction that Eleanor Clarke had simply laughed at the law? Warner himself had taken the opposite point of view; remembering her apparent straight-forwardness, the honesty which seemed to emanate from her, Warner cursed himself for a fool. He felt that he would never be able to trust his own judgment again.

His fit of self-derision was brought to a close as the train arrived at the harbour station. It was nearly deserted at that hour, for the next boat did not go out until the evening and Warner had no difficulty in perceiving that Eleanor Clarke was not among the passengers who alighted. Sitting tight in his place, he pondered over the next move.

Would she go to Seaford and wile away the hours until it was time to get the boat? This time he was not left long in doubt. The next stop was at Bishopstone halt, and here Eleanor Clarke alighted on the little country platform and walked straight to the exit. There was no one in charge at the halt,—the guard collected tickets from any passengers who got out there, and of him Warner enquired if it were possible to get a car.

"Not here. Not until you get to Seaford, sir."

"How long will that take you?"

"A matter of three minutes, sir."

"Send a taxi back from the station to pick me up on the main road outside here—as fast as you can."

With that Warner hastened down the narrow path which led from the halt to the main road. Racking his brains to recall his whereabouts, he remembered that the road they were approaching was that which ran between Brighton, Newhaven and Eastbourne,—a road well served by 'buses, and he hastened his steps a little, lest he were left in the lurch again. If Eleanor Clarke got on a 'bus, he hoped his taxi would turn up in time to follow it. The train took three minutes to get to Seaford; reckoning seven minutes for the taxi to drive back, Warner felt fairly safe. She couldn't get very far in that time, and every minute the chances became better for him. But when she reached the main road, Eleanor Clarke did not stop to look for a 'bus. Instead, after following the road for a few hundred yards in the direction of Seaford, she turned off to the left along the bye-road which led to the village of Bishopstone. Warner, following a few hundred yards behind, couldn't help chuckling.

"She's one of these infinite resource and sagacity people. Is she going to lose me on the downs? Chase over the Seven Sisters. Exclusive! Special!"

A moment later Warner saw her turn into the lych-gate which led to the little Norman church round which clustered the red roofs of the tiny hamlet. Pausing, Warner wondered if there were a second gate to the churchyard; she was quite capable, he guessed, of climbing the churchyard wall and getting away on the further side. Presumably she knew the ground and certainly he did not. So Warner went in through the lych-gate, too, hoping he would not meet the lady face to face at the corner of the church. He still did not know if she realised that she was being followed; certainly she had not turned her head to look behind her, either in the rush across Brighton Station, nor yet since she had left the train. Loitering in the churchyard looking with unseeing eyes at the gravestones, Warner began to get perturbed. He had lost sight of her and he didn't like it. He decided to risk being seen and peered round the corner of the little apse. Still seeing nobody, he ventured cautiously round the east end and surveyed the other side of the churchyard.

"I'll bet she's slipped over the wall," he ruminated. "This is a mug's game. Seeing but not seen, likewise waiting at the church,—left me in the lurch,—oh, it did upset me… Hell! What's that?"

That was the sound of a car on the road outside.

"The same old game," said Warner, running to the lych-gate. Had he wished, he could have caught up with the car before it accelerated,—but he did not so wish.

"All in good time is a good motto," he chuckled, as he noted the number of the car and the fact that it had "Hackney carriage" inscribed on a plate at the rear. "Now if only that guard has done his bit, this ought to be the last lap," he meditated as he ran towards the main road. The guard had done as he was asked, and a taxi stood a little way down the main road.

"You were sent out by the guard at Seaford station," said Warner to the taxi driver. "I want to follow a car that has just come out from the Bishopstone turning. It was a taxi, number XX2259."

"That's me brother's taxi," said the driver as Warner jumped on to the seat beside him. "I saw him two minutes ago. He's driving towards Eastbourne."

"Get a move on and try and catch sight of him," said Warner, "but don't get too close and don't try to pass him."

"Pass him? In this?" retorted the other. "Likely, eh? He's got a brand new Austin, and this is a 1920 Buick. I can follow him all right. They all know us in Seaford, we shall soon hear what road he's taken."

They ran along Seaford front and turned up by the station. Here the driver shouted to the man on point duty.

"Seen Garge pass?"

With a gesture the constable pointed over his shoulder.

"He took the Eastbourne road, matter of three minutes ago."

The ancient car rattled on again furiously. A moment later, at a fork in the road, the resourceful driver shouted to a van driver.

"Seen Garge pass?"

"Yep. Eastbourne Road."

"That's all right, sir. That's easy now. We shan't catch him, but we shall see him ahead as he goes up the hill above Exeat. I hope my tin kettle won't boil though. Shockin' hills these. I don't often try to hurry her up them."

Watching the road ahead Warner couldn't help admiring the loveliness of the rolling downland. Descending to the Cuckmere valley they crossed an awkward little iron bridge and a moment later the driver pointed to a car which appeared on the crest of the hill that mounted in front of them.

"That's Garge. He's just passing Friston Church."

Warner felt hopeful; the distance between the cars was not great, but the old Buick toiled up the steep slope of the downs at a funeral rate, her engine rattling as though with distress. It seemed as though they must stop before the summit, but the car with a cough and a back fire somehow jerked itself on to the level. A "Southdown" 'bus running in the Seaford direction, stood by the pond which reflected the little church on the summit of the hill and once again Warner heard the formula shouted.

"Seen Garge?" and the 'bus driver called back, "Passed him up Eastdean hill."

"All aboard," chuckled the taxi man, "we're all right. Lovely cars them new Austins, runs as sweet as honey."

"Were you in the garage when the order came for your brother to go to Bishopstone?" asked Warner.

"Not me! My garage is in Seaford. Garge is in New'aven. Serves the boat trains."

"Does he, by Jove!" thought Warner. "Well there's plenty of time for the boat. She doesn't sail till 6.30."

"You know there's a bit of a snag further on," confided the driver a minute later. "There's two roads into Eastbourne. One by Old Town, one down into Meads. Unless we have an uncommon bit of luck we shan't know which he's taking."

Warner sat and considered the matter; it certainly was a snag, and he knew by this time that any hope of catching up with the Austin was gone. He wondered if he would do better to stop another car and ask for a lift in the hope of catching up. Suggesting this to the driver, the latter replied, "Just as you like, sir, but you won't do it. Garge'll be into Eastbourne now." Just as they ran along the level again on the further side of Eastdean hill, there was a sudden loud report and the Buick swerved over into the middle of the road.

"That's torn it," said the driver. "Tyre burst."

Warner jumped out and looked back along the road. The first car which passed ignored his signal and raced by on the far side of the road, the next was an aged Ford making no speed at all, and then the matter was clinched by a cry from the driver.

"There's Garge, sir. He's coming back!"

Jumping into the middle of the road, the Seaford driver hailed his brother.

"Cops!" he said succinctly, pointing to Warner. "Wants your fare. Where did you drop her?"

Garge scratched his head. "Old Town church," he replied promptly.

"What did the lady do when you dropped her?" asked Warner.

"Walked orf, sir. Just down the road. She might ha' got a 'bus—or she mightn't. I dunno."

"I think you'd better run me into Eastbourne," said Warner, "we've been trailing you from Bishopstone." He paid the driver of the Buick and jumped into the Austin.

"How did you get that order to go to Bishopstone?" he enquired as they set out again.

"Trunk call," replied Garge. "Lady rang me up about half past two and told me to be outside Bishopstone church at five o'clock and no mistake about it. I went all right. People don't go slinging trunk calls for nix. She asked me to step on it,—and I did."

"You certainly did," replied Warner. "I might have done better if I'd changed cars at Seaford and got into something that could move."

"Wouldn't have made no difference, sir. There's hardly a car on hire in the place that could ha' done it. It's only took me a spot over quarter of an hour. By the time you'd got another car I should ha' been there."

"I thought of all that," said Warner. "You can get a good speed out of this one."

"Sixty's nothing to 'er," replied the proud owner, "and she just eats them hills."

At Old Town church, on the first rise of the downs above Eastbourne, Warner stopped and asked the man on point duty if he had seen where Garge's fare went when she left the Austin. The constable thought she had taken a 'bus into the town; he had noticed the Austin pull up and remembered the young woman walking down the hill.

"Police Station," said Warner promptly to Garge, and again they set out.

Arrived there, Warner spent an energetic ten minutes explaining his errand and giving descriptions of the object of his search. Then he turned to the sergeant in charge with the twinkle which made him so likeable.

"I know that looking for visitors in Eastbourne is like looking for a needle in a haystack, but I've got an idea there's a couple staying in the place whom I want badly. The man is a tall fellow, aged about fifty, greyish-haired, clean-shaven. His wife is about the same age; dark, stoutish, brown eyes, square face. They've been staying here since April 19th, or thereabouts."

"Well, that's a funny thing," said the sergeant. "Name of Edwards?"

"Maybe," said Warner. "I don't know what name they'll go by and I've never seen either of them. The woman,—if my guess is right—is the housekeeper in the Lestrange case. The girl I've been trailing is the secretary. What's funny about it, and who are the Edwards?"

"Man and wife, just the age and appearance you describe, been staying at a boarding house in Meads since April 19th," reeled off the sergeant. "Their car collided with a lorry outside the station yesterday. The wife was killed outright, the man was alive when they got him to hospital, but he's dying—can't last more than a few hours they say. A shocking smash it was. He must have got mixed up between his brake and accelerator,—the lorry simply crumpled them up…"

"Where's the hospital?" demanded Warner.

"The Princess May Hospital,—I'll come with you if you think it's worth while."

"I should say it was certainly worth while," said Warner. "I expect we shall find Miss Clarke there, too."

The sergeant's eyes fairly goggled.

"They say the poor chap can't last the night out," he said regretfully, but Warner replied, "So much the better for him. He'd certainly have hung if he's the man I think him."

CHAPTER XVI

WHEN WARNER ARRIVED AT THE PRINCESS MAY HOSPITAL he asked to see the Matron; giving her his official card, he said that it was necessary for him to see Mr. Edwards.

She looked at him in some astonishment, and then said,

"You must understand quite clearly that the man is dying. Whatever you want him for makes no difference—his death is only a matter of hours. He has one visitor with him already,—a Miss Clarke. I wrote to her for him yesterday evening and I think his one desire was to live until she arrived. He is dictating something to her with his nurse as a witness. Presumably you will be willing to wait until she has finished what he wants done?"

"I think it is my duty to go straight to him," replied Warner. "Don't think I am inhuman; the law is powerless in the presence of death, but while the man is still alive it's my business to see if I can identify him."

"Very well. I will take you up," she replied.

When the Matron opened the door of the private room in which lay the dying man, she stopped and made a gesture indicating that Warner should stay still by the door. Looking at the face of the man in the bed, Warner knew that no questions would ever be answered by him again. The strong featured face showed already the nobility of death. A doctor stood on the further side of the bed, a nurse beside him, and Eleanor Clarke sat by the pillow, her head bent as she leaned forward and watched the still face.

The doctor leaving the bedside, came towards the Matron and said in a low voice,

"The effort he made was too much for him. He died just as you came into the room."

Warner went softly out of the room and said to the Matron when she followed him a moment later,

"I'm afraid I shall have to wait and see Miss Clarke. Will you guarantee that she does not leave the building before I have spoken to her?"

The Matron looked at him with cold disapproval.

"Very well," she replied. "I suppose if it is a police matter I am bound to do as you ask."

"I'm afraid you are," said Warner, "and I am bound to do my job, but I'll do it as decently as I can."

It was less than half an hour later that the door of the small room in which he was waiting opened, and Eleanor Clarke, as self-controlled as ever, entered.

"I am sorry that I gave you the slip in that very underhand manner," she said quietly, "but Mr. Lestrange had always been very kind to me. Just before you telephoned to me, I had a letter from the Matron here. It came by the half-past twelve post. Perhaps you would like to read it."

Warner took the letter she held out and read,

"Madam,

"I am asked to write to you by a Mr. Edwards who is in this hospital, dying from injuries received in a motor accident. He says that you knew him as Mr. Thomas

Browne, and he begs that you will come here to see
him immediately, as he cannot live for more than a day
or two. He says that he wishes to make an explanation
to you of recent events. His words to me were—'Ask
her to come alone, she will understand. I want to die in
peace.'…"

Warner handed back the letter and she went on in her level voice.
"I knew you were following me. I did what I did in the hope of
giving Mr. Lestrange his wish. The letter from the Matron said
he was dying, so it couldn't have made any difference to you,
but if you had followed on my heels here it would have made
a lot of difference to him. I'm quite willing to 'come quietly' as
the saying is, if you have any charge to make against me, but
I'm quite unrepentant."

Warner suddenly smiled. "There's no charge against you
for giving me the slip," he said, "but I've got to know what happened,—that Saturday night at Temple Grove."

Once again she held out a paper. "Can you read shorthand?
In any case the nurse who was a witness will be able to tell
you that what I have written is a true account of what he
said."

"I'm not very good at reading anyone's shorthand but my
own," replied Warner, "and I'm not too good at that, but
I'm willing to tell you my own guess at the solution of the
Lestrange conundrum, and you can tell me if I have guessed
right."

"I don't see how you could guess," she retorted.

"You think we're awful fools, don't you?" said Warner, without a trace of resentment in his pleasant voice. "You see for a

long time I made the mistake of assuming that Michael Ashe killed Vivian Lestrange. Instead of which, Vivian Lestrange killed Michael Ashe. Is that right?"

She nodded. "Yes. It's all explained here."

"You just listen to me for a minute," said Warner. "You owe me a little consideration after that dance you led me. Vivian Lestrange was once called Edward Merstham and Michael Ashe was his brother James.

"Michael Ashe found Lestrange because he traced you to your home after that famous dinner party at Marriott's."

"You're wrong there," she replied. "Mr. Lestrange realised that Ashe was his brother through something in one of Michael Ashe's books. He telephoned to him at the Addison Club that Saturday evening and asked him to come and call on the real Vivian Lestrange."

"Well, that isn't a large discrepancy," replied Warner. "When Ashe arrived, Lestrange shot him, put the body—with Mrs. Fife's assistance—into Ashe's car (in which he had driven to Temple Grove) and later Lestrange drove the car to Ross and put the body in the fireplace at Kirkham Barns. Lestrange's subsequent actions were all calculated to foster the impression that it was he himself who was the victim."

Eleanor Clarke nodded. "Yes. You're quite right," she replied, and Warner could hear the weariness behind the quiet voice. "You have every reason for feeling satisfied," she went on, "I suppose this is what you would call a successful case,—except that you can't hang the murderer."

"Believe me or believe me not, I hate hangings," replied Warner, "if only out of consideration for the hangman I'd gladly have them abolished. In this case the score is paid…"

Silence fell between them for a little while and then the Chief Inspector said,

"You are tired and upset after all this agitation,"—but she cut him short.

"That doesn't matter. I want a typewriter to type this statement, and then you can read it to the nurse who acted as witness. After that I should be glad to go back home,—unless you find it necessary to detain me down here."

"Go back home by all means," replied Warner. "To the best of my knowledge we have nothing against you,—I don't believe for an instant that you knew anything more about the case than you told us."

She looked at him quickly. "I should like to thank you," she said suddenly, "because you believed me when I told you the truth. I did realise that it was a difficult truth for you to believe."

Warner laughed a little. "Everyone has a modicum of conceit," he rejoined. "I did believe you, but honesty compels me to admit that I did a bit of Thomas-ing at moments. If it had turned out that I had been absolutely wrong in believing you, it would have been a nasty shock to my *amour propre.* As it is, right or wrong, I feel that my judgment has been vindicated—pro tem… Is that another instance of what you would call male conceit?"

She flashed a laugh at him. "Neither conceit nor ability is a purely masculine monopoly," she replied primly. "We're a mixed lot, all of us!"

CHAPTER XVII

VIVIAN LESTRANGE'S STATEMENT WAS A MODEL OF LUCID-
ity, and Warner, as he passed it to Bond on the following
day, said,

"If my brain functions as well as that when I'm dying I shall
die proud and happy. The poor beggar's explained everything
with a minimum of fuss."

Bond sat with knitted brows over the typed sheets.

"My real name is Edward Merstham," began the statement. "In 1924 I was imprisoned for a fraud manipulated
by my brother James, who managed to escape arrest. I
swore then that I would kill him before I died.

"After seven years in Parkhurst I was liberated and
then went to live with a woman named Alice Latimer,
who had in past years suffered at the hands of my brother
James. She was a very good woman and she kept me
until I began to earn money by writing. Two years ago I
read *Allen of the Andamans*, by Michael Ashe, and realised
that the name Michael Ashe covered the identity of my
brother James.

"Through the integrity of two women—Mrs. Fife and
Miss Clarke—I was enabled to conceal my real identity
and to plan out James's death in a manner that seemed
to ensure my own safety.

"On Saturday, April 14th, I telephoned to Michael Ashe at his club, asking him to call that evening on the real Vivian Lestrange. He had no idea of my identity, and came, and I shot him the moment he entered the room. I placed his body in his own car which stood outside my gate and ran the car into the yard next door, knowing that my neighbours were away. In the car I found James's typewriter and on his body a letter which I posted later to his publishers in an envelope which I had obtained through the post from Genoa. With Mrs. Fife's assistance I tidied up the house at Temple Grove and made a hole in the window to indicate a shot. I myself drove James's car, containing his body, to Kirkham on Saturday night. Mrs. Fife met me there and assisted in the disposal of the remains. I hoped that my pocket-book, which I left on the body, would be identified. I drove the car on Sunday night and through the early hours of Monday morning to Ross and to Southampton and garaged it there. After that I rejoined Mrs. Fife in a boarding house in Eastbourne where we were known as Mr. and Mrs. Edwards, having stayed there before. I sent a packet of Treasury notes to Miss Clarke, using James's typewriter, and also sent a letter to the police referring to Vivian Lestrange's death. I counted on the fact that the police would arrive at the conclusion that Michael Ashe killed Vivian Lestrange.

"The only person who knew anything at all of the facts here set forth was Mrs. Fife. She is already dead, and this statement cannot harm her."

In addition to this statement was a copy of another paper.

> "This is the last Will and Testament of me Edward
> Merstham, known also as Vivian Lestrange, Author. I
> leave everything of which I die possessed and any royalties
> which may accrue to me under my pen name of Vivian
> Lestrange to Eleanor Clarke, of Clare Court.
>
> "I appoint the said Eleanor Clarke as my literary execu-
> tor, giving her power to deal with any or all of my MSS.
> as she thinks fit."

"So that's that," said Bond. "I was wrong about the young woman
all through. It was her confounded glibness put me off..."

"She was one of the most difficult people to assess whom I
ever encountered," said Warner. "It was obvious that she saw
further in front of her nose than most people, and that very
clarity of thought seemed to make for suspicion. It's odd that
in our job the very fact of a person being always in the right and
hastening to do the right thing makes us look askance at them.
Eleanor Clarke is the perfect secretary, she's never at a loss under
any circumstances. You've got one satisfaction out of this case,
Bond,—and that was the toothbrush. That toothbrush would
have been the determining factor if events hadn't rushed to a
head as they did."

Bond shrugged his shoulders.

"How could the toothbrush have led you to Vivian Lestrange,
when you were looking for Michael Ashe, sir?" he asked.

"It's easy to be wise after the event," replied Warner, "but
whether you believe me or not, it's a fact that when I followed
Eleanor Clarke to Sussex, it was in the hope that I should find

Vivian Lestrange at the end of the trail, and not Michael Ashe.
The evidence for Ashe's existence depended on two factors—
the typewriter and the Genoa letter. If Ashe went in his car to
Temple Grove the typewriter would almost certainly have been
in the car with his other luggage. I ought to have realised that
earlier. Ashe was intending to travel and he would never have
travelled without his typewriter,—no author ever does. So that
if Ashe were killed at Temple Grove, the typewriter would
have fallen into the hands of his murderer. Now for the Genoa
letter. The letter was genuine,—Ashe had actually written it.
The postmarks were genuine, too,—but the envelope did not
originally have the typed address to Langston's on it. I should
imagine that Lestrange wrote to some hotel in Genoa, enclos-
ing an envelope for reply, addressed in ordinary ink. When
he received the letter with its Italian stamp and cancelling, he
bleached out the written address with ordinary ink eradicator,
steamed open the flap, inserted the letter from Ashe, stuck
it up again, and then typed the publisher's address when the
envelope was dry. After that he dropped it into the letter-box
at Langston's. It was a very convincing piece of evidence. The
letter was genuine, the postmark ditto, and the typing was the
final touch." Warner smiled here. "The detecting in Vivian
Lestrange's novels may have been a different sort of affair from
our humdrum ways here, but he was very acute over human
nature. He guessed the typing would be noticed, he was certain
the letter itself and the postmark would be examined by experts
and he thought the sum total of these effects would cause so
much cerebral excitement on our part that we would take the
thing for granted, and he wasn't far wrong. He had brains, had
Vivian Lestrange."

Bond sat frowning a little, still looking at the typed sheets in front of him.

"Lestrange did a bit of jumping to conclusions when he assumed that we should connect up Michael Ashe with the Temple Grove affair, sir," he said. "How could he have told that Michael Ashe would ever come under our notice?"

"Lestrange paid us the compliment of believing that we'd do our part of the job properly," said Warner. "He laid a trail and laid it well, without over emphasising anything. He knew that enquiries would be made at Kirkham, and guessed that we might cotton on to the Merstham story, and he probably hoped that Ashe's car had been noticed in the neighbourhood. Taking it all into consideration he did the thing well, and assumed that our routine enquiries would be pretty thorough. In fact, the only point where he overacted his part was in that 'Penal Product letter.' His insistence that Vivian Lestrange was dead was a spot overdone. It eventually awoke in my mind a conviction that Vivian Lestrange was not dead at all."

Bond suddenly grinned.

"Your scepticism was justified, sir, while mine was not," he said, but Warner replied,

"The essence of detection is scepticism—or at least agnosticism. No taking things on faith without facts in our line of business, Bond."

THE END

ALSO AVAILABLE

Crime author Dick Markham is in love again; his fiancée is the mysterious newcomer to the village, Lesley Grant. When Grant accidentally shoots the fortune teller through the side of his tent at the local fair—following a very strange reaction to his predictions—Markham is reluctantly brought into a scheme to expose his betrothed as a suspected serial husband-poisoner.

That night the enigmatic fortune teller—and chief accuser—is found dead in an impossible locked-room setup, casting suspicion onto Grant and striking doubt into the heart of her lover. Lured by the scent of the impossible case, Dr Gideon Fell arrives from London to examine the perplexing evidence and match wits with a meticulous killer at large.

First published in 1944, *Till Death Do Us Part* remains a pacey and deeply satisfying impossible crime story, championed by Carr connoisseurs as one of the very best examples of his mystery writing talents.

ALSO AVAILABLE
IN THE BRITISH LIBRARY
CRIME CLASSICS SERIES

Many of our titles are also available
in eBook, large print and audio editions